DODGING SHELLS

SHELLS

W.L. Bertsch

Ocean Highway Books ™

Independent Publishing Consultants

For my dad . . . Thomas Henry Smith

Also by this author:

Once More, From the Beginning

Table of Contents

July 19, 1943   1

July 29, 1943   15

August 8, 1943   34

August 18, 1943   39

August 27, 1943   50

October 2, 1943   57

October 10, 1943   75

November 13, 1943   87

December 18, 1943   109

January 10, 1944   116

February 19, 1944   126

April 6, 1944   140

June 3, 1944   155

July 20, 1944   169

September 30, 1944   177

November 10, 1944   187

November 22, 1944   191

November 27, 1944   195

Other Books by This Author

ACKNOWLEDGEMENT

Thanks to my editor, Bob Crickard, for his enthusiasm and good advice.

July 19, 1943

Kath,

Let me start by saying I'm fine now. It's not as bad as it sounds. And it wasn't my fault.

I got shot. Yes, shot. In the back. Before we even *landed* in Sicily.

You always said I'd come to an embarrassing end, and I damn near did! It's that kind of insight that makes it such fun to have a twin sister.

In fact, I may have been the very first Allied casualty in the entire invasion. You can start knitting a suitable battle decoration to send over. I'll pin it on my shirt. I'm not counting on receiving anything official.

When the 48th Highlanders were finally shipping out to fight in Sicily (we didn't know where we were headed at the time, of course) the Brits scrounged all over until they found us the crappiest vessel in the entire British navy. It was a worn out piece of junk called the Derbyshire, and it had been used to transport troops to the East Indies in peacetime. The deck space that was usually taken up by lifeboats had been filled with assault landing craft and they had generously reserved one hold especially for us.

Rows of scarred wooden benches and trestle tables piled with our kit filled it, wall to wall. Our hammocks were slung over the tables, and life preservers did double duty as pillows. Except for a few minutes exercise on deck from time to time, we spent most of the trip down there. We ate there, we slept there, and we passed the rest of our time right there—playing cards, smoking and placing swaggering bets on our intended destination. It was cramped, it was depressing, and it smelled bad. For all I could see, we could have been cruising aimlessly around and around the British Isles the whole time. At night, the hammocks filled the space so anybody unfortunate enough to need to take a leak had to push other sleepers aside on his way to the head. This was not a popular move.

What's the 'head', you ask? Well, it was much like a communal outhouse—urinals along one side, and holes perched over the scuppers where the water could wash away whatever fell. There was no privacy, and nobody hung around in there any longer than they had to.

While we were trapped aboard this floating slum, the British naval officers found several creative little ways to punish us landlubbers for the inconvenience we were causing by just being there.

One of those fine officers stopped by to give us our first bit of good news. "Between 0800 and 1100 hours, you will leave the area below decks." This was so the housecleaning crew could work its magic.

"Hey, that's great!" We were delighted. "We can get some fresh air on deck and enjoy the view." If there *was* any view.

"Certainly not!"

"Why the hell not?"

"The deck must be kept available at all times for physical training."

"You're kidding!" He didn't look like he was kidding.

"Oh…and there will be no loitering on the gangways," he added.

We were baffled. "What do you expect us to do—swim alongside the damn' ship?" He ignored this anonymous mutter and made no other suggestions. Maybe he figured that was as good a solution as any.

So for three hours a day we were on the move, restlessly wandering back and forth along the gangways—killing time, cursing all sea-going vessels and this sorry example in particular. We couldn't see a speck of rust anywhere, mind you: steel walls, steel ceilings and steel floors, and every scrap of it hidden under about a hundred layers of paint, all grey. It was like living inside a restless boiler room.

Kitchen patrol was another sneaky form of torture. It's no big deal to carry a hundred pound sack of flour up the ladder out of the hold—if you know how. But ships bob up and down with the waves. If the ship is headed down while you're climbing up, those one hundred pounds become about two hundred pounds temporarily, and every sailor on board gets to enjoy a good laugh at your expense. Here's the trick: you have to time it so you dash up while the ship is on the rise, then grab the top rung and hang on like grim death for the down stroke. When you get a second lift, you can heave yourself and your cargo up and onto the deck. Believe me, Sis, you're going to want to remember this tip if you're ever expected to haul flour in a ship.

But the lowest trick of all came when breakfast was served—with suspicious, oily fish things.

Silence fell. "Those look like kippers," I said. Somebody had to.

"They *are* kippers," replied the sailor who had brought them in.

"But we don't *eat* kippers...and if we did, we sure wouldn't eat them for *breakfast*. They're disgusting!"

"Aw, you blokes don't know what's good."

"Well, *we won't eat them*, will we, guys?" Three hundred fellow Canadians backed me up. We wouldn't eat them—not a chance!

"Suit yourselves, mates." Apparently the menu was not negotiable. We went hungry that morning...but the torture didn't end there. The fetid odour of those kippers had seeped into every nook and cranny of the hold. And it clung like fungus. It was hard enough on a healthy man, but god only knows how the guys who were suffering from seasickness survived it.

There *was* a canteen on board, with candy bars and stuff for anybody with a bit of spare cash. What a lifesaver for a bunch of hungry guys who had been refused a decent morning meal! Unfortunately, we didn't *have* any cash. None at all. Remember, we were going into battle. We'd conscientiously spent all our money on shore before boarding this little corner of hell. Who could have guessed we'd need it?

"What in hell kind of raw deal is this?" we bitched. (We did a lot of bitching aboard the Derbyshire; it seemed tailor-made for bitching.) But they couldn't get *us* down. We would wait, murmuring curses under our breath, till payday. Then we'd snap up every goddam Hershey bar aboard this tub, and hog them all for ourselves!

On payday, we prowled along the gangways, waiting to get our revenge. At eleven hundred hours, the money was distributed, and we flocked to the canteen. It was closed.

A passing seaman gave us the news. "Sorry, chaps. Canteen closes at ten hundred hours."

"But we just got paid! Just now!"

"Bad luck, blokes. It'll be open tomorrow. Save your coppers till then."

"C'mon! Give us a break!"

"Can't be done. Regulations, y'know."

We knew they were getting a big kick out of this first-rate joke on the poor simple Canadians. Those guys didn't know who they were dealing with. A few days later, an indignant British naval officer appeared in the hold flanked by two cocky little Limey sailors equipped with great long bayonets. We were not impressed.

"A considerable amount of material appears to have been stolen out of the ship's armouries. This is not only unacceptable. It is criminal! Does anyone here know anything about this outrage?"

Nobody knew a thing. "Are you sure it hasn't been misplaced, sir? By accident?"

No response.

"What all is missing, sir? Maybe we could help search."

"Oh, ammunition... tracer bullets... you know very well what's missing!"

"Wow! Tracer bullets and everything. That's really tough, sir! *We* don't even *get* tracer bullets..." Tracer bullets glow so you can see where they are going. They're used to adjust trajectory, but they weren't issued to the Canadian troops—at least, not to us. They're probably considered way too much fun.

"See here—we know you took them." His face had gone all red and blotchy. I thought he was going to have a fit or something. "You'd better return the lot, and quickly, or I'll put you *all* on report! Nobody gets off this ship until every last thing is returned!" Ignoring the sarcastic cheer that followed this hollow threat, he stalked out. His two tiny henchmen attempted a stalk, but it wasn't very effective. They didn't have the height for it.

Too bad. He missed hearing several creative suggestions about what he could do with the missing stuff once he found it.

"He sure told *us*, boy!" Nobody was taking this official crap very seriously. We didn't think much of the officer's high-handed attitude, and his bantam buddies? Well, they were just comical.

"Fancy him suspecting we were involved! I'm hurt. Really hurt."

"How can they think we'd do such a thing...and right under their bloody British noses?"

We had a good laugh, and then one of our own officers stood up. "All right, that's enough, guys. You've had your fun. Exactly how are you stupid sons of bitches planning to haul all that extra weight?" A few grins faded.

"Now, I'm going to spread a couple of ground sheets down on the deck...here. You can either put any contraband on there, and I'll return it…or you can damn' well try to carry it all past the Germans." He sauntered out.

A whole lot of stuff hit those sheets before he came back in—ammunition, machine guns, grenades, tracer bullets—almost as much as what had gone missing. Almost.

Sounds all safe as swimming pools, doesn't it? Well, they'd provided an escort of corvettes and maybe one or two destroyers to see that we got to land in shape to do the enemy some damage. But at least one German U-boat commander must have been braver or more short-sighted than the rest, because he got close enough to give us a scare.

Boom!

"Shit! What the hell was *that*?" Three hundred men immediately lost interest in whatever they were doing at the time.

"Was that thunder?" someone wondered, hopefully. Not all of us welcomed this explanation. A storm at sea. Wonderful.

Boom! Boom! The concussions quivered the air in the hold like the inside of a big base drum.

"Sounds like we've been hit!" We listened for the sound of water rushing through the gangways and I, for one, tried a quick guess at the temperature of the sea at this time of the year somewhere between Scotland and our secret mystery destination. I had absolutely no idea, but I was afraid I was going to find out. And soon.

We'd started to think they were going to let us sink with the rats that were too lame or stupid to leave the ship, when a sailor popped his head into the hold. We must have been a sorry, cowering sight.

"We're just dropping depth charges on a U-boat, mates. Best to keep them at a distance, you know. Sounds rather fine in here, though, doesn't it? Don't worry—we'll let you know if we get hit."

He grinned and popped out again. He couldn't wait to join his seafaring chums in mocking the poor dumb Canadians.

After we'd been on board for many days—way too many days, if you ask me—they told us we were finally getting into The Big Game. We were heading to Sicily to battle the Hun, and after bloody *years* of training in England, it was about time! We were primed to take on the entire German army, and we wanted to get on with it.

We were called up before dawn. The latrine was doing a brisk business. Seeing the number of guys heading in that direction, you'd have thought they were screening a major Hollywood flick in there! Pre-battle nerves seem to have that effect on the guys, loosening bowels and bladders all 'round. It was even drawing repeat customers, with some fellows going back three or four times. I won't say we were afraid...but if you've ever wondered where the phrase 'scared shitless' came from—well, now you know!

Even those who had no such problem wanted to get this particular essential piece of business over with before the order to prepare for landing. Nobody wanted to be caught short at an inconvenient time and place—and the beach we were headed for was going to be a damned inconvenient place!

By first light, the ship was manoeuvring into position for the assault landing and we were pumped up for the fight, adjusting our gear and checking our weapons, waiting for them to call our landing craft number. A bunch of Royal Marines were grouped along one side of the hold: British Marine Commandos. I don't know why they had been put in there with us—I guess it was the most convenient bit of space available—but their number had been called and they were grabbing up their stuff, ready to move out.

In the middle of all the confusion I heard a crack and felt a searing pain in my back.

What the hell? I reached back, and my hand came away bloody. "You've been shot!" I heard someone say. "He's been shot!"

Shit! *Shit!* I was going to be left behind! (I was pretty sure I wasn't dying.) All the drilling…all the work…all that *time*…I was *ready!* And now I was going to miss all the action!

A space had cleared around a startled-looking Marine, and it was clear—to me, at least—that he was the culprit. I catapulted across the hold and grabbed him by the collar.

"You sonofabitch…you shot me!"

The guy sort of stood there with his eyes wide and his mouth shut and let me shake him. He may have been a little frightened—I don't know—but he could hardly fight back, could he? I mean, he'd just *shot* me, for Chrissake! I don't know what I hoped to do about it—strangle him, maybe—but I felt hands grabbing at me, pulling at my shirt to see the damage.

"Wait, Smitty…wait. This is no bullet hole. Let's see it…"

Somehow, that took a bit of the drama out of it. I let go of the Marine, and his buddies hustled him out to their landing craft before more harm could be done.

Turns out it wasn't serious. The guy must have been fiddling around with his rifle…and dropped it. Stupid bastard! The gun fired, the bullet hit the metal deck, and a steel fragment found my back—or maybe it was a piece of the bullet. My closest pals were quick to voice their relief, in their own special way:

"C'mon Smitty…you gotta know we've all wanted to do that for ages! He was only the first one to get around to it."

"You're lucky he wasn't as good a shot as we are, or you'd be in a lot worse shape."

"Yeah, if he'd known you as well as we do, he'd have taken better aim!"

A couple of the officers wanted to put me in the hospital, but it was only a very *little* hole. I convinced them it wasn't much more than a scratch.

"Just tape it up. I'm fine." Then I forgot all about it.

That's a lucky thing, because if I'd been looking for sympathy, I was in the wrong place. We were moving out, and every one of those three hundred guys had a lot of more important things to think about.

DODGING SHELLS

When our own number was finally called, about thirty-five of us swarmed up out of the hold and onto a landing craft, which darted toward the beach. All the time we had waited, waited, waited to land, Allied shells had been pounding hell out of the area. We hoped nobody was left on shore to object to our arrival.

The assault landing craft was one of those big motorized barges; no deck, only a flat bottom full of soldiers, with three sides and a snub front that would drop down to form a ramp when we neared the shore. We would charge down it and splash through knee-deep water to reach the beach—if we were lucky. If the pilot got it wrong, the craft would ram right up onto the beach and get hopelessly stuck or, much worse for us, let us off in deeper water, where we'd have to plough through as best we could, trying to keep our weapons dry, with forty pounds of gear and our soaking uniforms weighing us down.

We were lucky, as it happened...and we would have been grateful, too, if we'd had time.

There was no chance that we could arrive unnoticed by any defenders that might be lurking about. The Beachmaster, a navy guy, was shining a bloody *beacon* onto the sand, showing us where to land, and bellowing, "You...*here*. You...*over there!*" They may just as well have put up a placard for the enemy soldiers: "Gala beach assault—here today! Good targets still available." At least, that's how it struck me at the time.

There was little time to think, and no need. Our instructions were simple, and they'd been drilled into us: "Get off the beach! Never mind how many casualties you have…don't stop for anything. *Get off the beach!"*

Well, we did exactly what we'd been told. We hit the beach running and we didn't stop until we reached our objective—three miles inland. I saw no sign of the Italian army and the Jerries must have been sleeping off their breakfast knockwurst when we passed through, because we didn't run into any resistance. None. Oh, we heard shots, but there was nobody in our path to slow us down, so we kept right on going.

Well, we're finally here, we thought. *We're spearheading this invasion…we'd better not make asses of ourselves.* Our orders were to take the airfield. So we charged across it, as neat as you like, and kept right on going up to the heights on the other side. Others stayed to hold the ground we had so gallantly conquered. Our job was done. We were ready for dinner.

I dug into my Nifty Compact 24-Hour Ration Pack and extracted a can of soup. It doesn't sound like much, but that can was magic. You hit it a sharp tap on the top, and it warms *itself!* No kidding! And, like that wasn't enough:

"Look guys! The Germans are putting on a free fireworks display, and here we are with balcony seats!"

"Hey…anybody got popcorn?" Nobody had popcorn. Tea…a few candies…some chewing gum. But no popcorn.

The ships and the beach were being strafed and bombed plenty by then. It lit up the night sky with flashes and sparks and throbbed like thunder. I suppose we should have felt worse for the guys who were down there taking the heat, but to tell you the truth, we were mostly just glad it wasn't us.

So, how do you think I'm doing so far? I think it's going pretty well: no pratfalls until now, and my first 'war wound' has almost been forgotten —unless, of course, I come across that Marine again...

Sis, since I've been overseas it seems like you and I have barely kept in touch.

It's my fault, I know. The past three years in England I've been working as hard as I could to learn what I had to know to keep myself alive and kill the bad guys. And the time I had for relaxing...well, I guess I might have gone a bit overboard. England is a far cry from Toronto the Good. The pubs are open early and late, and they're plenty eager to serve a guy as much alcohol as his money can buy. What's an innocent soldier to do?

I've been lazy about writing letters, and I don't blame you for following my lead. I know you're thinking about me. But I miss being able to talk to you, and it looks like writing is the best we're going to be able to do for a while yet. Guys don't talk much about personal things...you know? I'm here with a great bunch—I'd trust them to cover my back any day—but you were my best friend for sixteen years. I guess that's one of the drawbacks of having a twin—nobody else ever gets quite as close.

So write often and tell me everything. I'm starved for the taste of home, after three and a half years, and the short notes we've been trading aren't nearly enough. I don't know when I'll be able to get letters out to you, but I'll write them anyway. And sooner or later, they'll get yours through to me.

Take care. I'll be counting on you.

Love
Tommy

July 29, 1943

Happy Birthday to us!

(Imagine fanfare here…and maybe those razzy rolled up paper things that shoot out when you blow into them.)

I doubt that I'll find a way to celebrate my birthday here. God only knows what kind of crap we'll get for dinner. With my luck, it'll be the dreaded Haricot Oxtail Stew-In-A-Can. And I'd rather starve. That disgusting mess—with bones left in for good measure—must be brewed up by some Limey sadist, probably a sailor with a mean grudge against the infantry. We can't even give it away to starving Italians along the road. We've tried; they won't take it!

So I'm celebrating with you. Sort of a birthday party by proxy! Call it one of the fringe benefits of being a twin.

How does twenty feel on that side of the pond? I'm finding it as hot and grimy and uncomfortable over here as nineteen was. When I enlisted, I sure never thought I'd still be over here four years later. And, believe me, there've been moments when I've wondered why I was so damned enthusiastic about it. Hell, if mom had gone down to the enlistment office and told them I was only sixteen, the way she threatened, I'd only have left town and joined up somewhere else.

Is it too late to change my mind?

They say when we landed it was the Italian armed forces who met us. That may be why there seemed to be nobody there; seems like their hearts weren't really in it. The Americans were not so lucky. They came on shore a bit further west and they faced the Germans, who weren't nearly so shy about objecting to the intrusion. That would account for the fireworks show that night.

After the airfield was taken, we were supposed to keep on going up into the central mountains. But the Yanks were having a real bad time and hadn't been able to get off the beach fast enough to avoid getting pinned down by German armour. So our orders were changed. We were to cut behind the Jerries, attack them and force them to retreat. (Sounds real easy when you spit it out all at once like that, doesn't it?)

If we were going to beat it over to take the pressure off the Yanks, we would have to move fast, and that was easier said than done. It was quite a distance, and the ship carrying our shiny new trucks and heavy transport equipment had gone down at sea the day before the landing. The artillery wagons had made it, and some of us were able to bum a ride with them at least part of the way, but mostly we walked. Fast.

When we found any, we 'borrowed' trucks, donkeys, mules—anything that moved—from Italian civilians along the way. They didn't seem awfully eager to offer these items. I think they suspected (with good reason) that we wouldn't go to any trouble to return them. We considered this ungenerous, and took them anyway.

DODGING SHELLS

Once we got there, we didn't find much of anybody to attack. I'd like to think we looked so fierce that we *scared* the Germans away, but I suspect they might have retreated to avoid getting caught between us and the Yanks. In any case, our job was done. The Americans were able to get off the beach, and we swung back over where we were supposed to go in the first place and continued on into the mountains.

A couple of days later, we were on a mountain overlooking a small hill village when we spotted a couple of big German lorries crawling along the road below us. One of them was pulling an eighty-eight millimetre cannon. (That's a *big* bruiser.) They were about fifteen hundred yards below—way out of range for us to do each other any serious damage with machine guns—but our officer decided to post a guard to keep an eye on them anyway. He left my pal Alfie and me on a convenient ledge, where the view was good, to do the job while the rest of the platoon found a more comfortable spot to hunker down for a while...no doubt because we two were such superior quality military material. We watched quietly for a while, then:

"Hey," said Alfie. "Why don't we shoot some tracer bullets down there—shake them up a bit?"

"Tracer bullets? Where the hell would we get...?"

"Well, just let me look. I may be able to find a few..." He grinned a gap-toothed grin and winked, digging around in his gear.

"You're kidding. From the ship?"

"Where else? So why don't we try them out? Maybe we can hit something."

We started to fire. The day was overcast, so we could see the patterns the tracers made against the dusty green hillside and the dusty brown road. As long as we didn't hit too close, the Jerries paid no attention. But when we got their range and the bullets started to kick up the dirt at their feet, they scattered like mice. We did a little war dance and pretended we'd routed a key element in the German defence plan. Turns out they hadn't gone far.

Ack-ack-ack-ack-ack. Big chunks of hillside flew up into the air around us. The tracer bullets had given away our location, and the Germans were pissed off. And they had anti-aircraft guns. We kind of wished we'd noticed *that!*

"What the hell are you *doing* over there, you stupid bastards?" That sounded like our lieutenant's holler, and he didn't sound very impressed.

"Um, we're ok, sir. Do you want us back there?"

"No. You stirred them up; now you stay there and keep an eye on them! But quit wasting ammunition. Did I see tracers?"

"No, sir."

We each dug in behind whatever cover looked most secure and watched patiently for a while. But the firing had stopped, everything was quiet, and crouching behind a rock isn't as exciting as it might sound.

"Alf," I called over to him, after a while. "I'm out of cigarettes. You got any?"

"Sure."

"I'm coming over." I sprinted over, at a crouch. Halfway along, bullets started slamming into the rocks around me, but none came too close. The Germans were shooting at anything that moved on that ledge.

I hunched up beside Alf, and lit the cigarette he offered.

"Enjoy your smoke," he said. "There's not enough cover here for both of us. I'm going over to where you were." He dashed over, and once again, the bullets began to gouge big chunks out of the hillside when he was about half way across. The Germans had dug in and were holding a grudge, but they were having trouble hitting a running target.

I finished my smoke and had been watching the Jerries do pretty much nothing at all for a while. "I think I might get a better view from over there at that other corner," I called to Alfie. "I'm going to have a look." I beat it over there, hearing the delayed *ack-ack-ack* of the guns starting up again.

"Is the view any better from there?" asked Alf, when I had reached my chosen site.

"Not really," I admitted.

Once I'd settled in, I yelled over, "Now it's your turn!"

It was great fun—sort of like the shooting gallery at the midway, except we were the ducks and the game was rigged so the suckers couldn't win. We kept sprinting from cover to cover, maybe firing a few shots along the way but with no real hope of doing any damage at all. We'd sometimes stop for a second along the way to do a brisk little dance step or make faces for the entertainment of our audience. (The rude gestures we made were more for our own enjoyment. We didn't expect the

Germans to find *them* amusing.) Every time the Jerries prepared to go on their way, we'd pop up somewhere on that ridge, and they couldn't resist trying another shot at us. We probably kept them busy there for about an hour or two. That should have been worth something.

Suddenly a shout: "You two get back off that ridge...it's not funny anymore!" It was the lieutenant again. "You're just drawing fire—somebody back here almost got shot!"

See how you get blamed for every little thing around here? Alfie and I seem to get blamed for more than our share...I wonder why?

You'd like Alf. His folks live over near Bathurst Street somewhere, but we didn't meet up until we reached England. I wasn't that impressed with him at the beginning; his curly blonde hair makes him look a bit too angelic, until he opens his mouth and that broken front tooth of his spoils the picture. It didn't take long to find out that we had a lot in common—he's used to making his own fun out of very little, like us, and he's game for just about anything.

But he clowns around a lot. I don't know what gets into him sometimes! I, on the other hand, am always very dignified. So the scrapes we're always getting into...they're all Alf's fault.

It seems like we Canadians are guarding the British 8th Army's entire left flank, all on our own. The Americans were supposed to be to the left of us all the way north through the mountains, but they must have found something better to do farther west because we haven't seen them at all. We never know *what* might be on our left, but whatever it is, it isn't singing Yankee Doodle. Maybe it's better this way, because roads are limited in the mountains, and the Yanks would have been sure to hog them. It's tough enough going already, with no transport. At least we don't need to skirt traffic jams all the way.

In fact, the only Americans we've seen the whole time were three paratroopers, and that wasn't intentional. They made a jump on a really windy day, aiming at some place entirely different, and they were blown all over the place. Three of them landed in our area by mistake and stayed with us for a while until they could rejoin their unit. They seemed like nice enough guys, but I didn't get to know them real well. We were on the move and couldn't spare a lot of time to be neighbourly.

We're not only fighting the Germans here in Sicily. We're fighting the Italian soldiers too, although the Italians are a lot slipperier. We rarely get a clear shot at them.

When we landed, they told us, "Any Italians with guns should be considered partisans. They don't like us. They're not our friends. They'll be looking for an opportunity to kill you, so don't take chances. Shoot all armed civilians." OK. No problem.

Well, one hot afternoon (they're all hot afternoons here) I was lying under cover on a hilltop, having a smoke and keeping an eye on a pathway below to make sure nothing dangerous came up on us by surprise. All of a sudden a moustachioed Italian appeared, trudging up the path and cradling a rifle in the crook of his arm.

Partisan! I jumped up and aimed my weapon directly at his chest. "Halt!" His hands flew up in the air, and the rifle hit the ground. That was just as well, because it was awkward, scrambling down that hill and keeping him covered while I did it. To be fair, it didn't look like he was planning to try anything rashly heroic.

Grabbing his gun—it was an old item; looked like it was only fit for shooting squirrels or whatever it is they hunt in their off hours over here—I let him know that he was now my prisoner. I herded him up the path toward my unit, thinking "*Damn*, I'm good! I've got this game right *down!*" I felt like a real veteran. In fact, I believe I grew three full inches before we got back to my platoon.

I have to say he didn't look like much, for a prisoner. He was a shortish, balding guy. He had food stains on his shirt front and was wearing some kind of sandal things. I would have preferred to capture something more menacing, but we don't always get to choose, do we?

On the way, we passed through a huddled collection of weathered stone hovels clinging to the hillside. He'd obviously been returning to his village...and this was it. Great. Word got around like wildfire and we accumulated a rustic retinue of women and children, all screeching and yammering in Italian. I ignored them altogether, which was easy because I couldn't understand a word they were saying.

When we reached camp, I marched him straight to the adjutant's tent, interrupting his conversation with several other officers who were gathered around, trying to make sense of one of the many completely unreliable Italian maps. I told him my story, as briefly as possible. (The looks on their faces told me I'd better stick to the short version.)

"...and I captured this partisan, sir."

They clearly had no time for this. "Right. Take him out and shoot him," snapped the adjutant.

I looked at him, stunned. "Well...I just captured him..."

"Yes...well, he's yours. You take him out...and shoot him. Those are your orders."

Feeling pretty crappy now, I stepped out of the tent into a crowd of about a *thousand* Italians, begging and wailing. (I'm guessing, here. I still couldn't understand them.) Grimy children clutched pathetically at my legs. This was really annoying.

They found someone to interpret for them. "Please," they were shrieking, "He was only out hunting!" A hundred or so of the littlest kids were sobbing, "Papa!"

I slunk back into the tent, and met several icy glares. "I think maybe he might not be a partisan after all." I felt like a fool. "These people say he was only out hunting."

"Can't you see we're busy?" snapped the adjutant. "Take the damn' guy out and shoot him! Now!"

I froze for a moment. I couldn't do *this*! I had to take a stand. "Look, *I'm* not going to shoot him ...you'll have to get somebody else to do it!"

A tent full of officers traded grim glances. "Well, in that case...break his rifle, kick him in the ass, and let him go."

As I stumbled out of the tent, I heard peals of laughter bouncing off the canvas walls and escaping through the door behind me. I haven't gone to any great bother to round up any more partisans.

It didn't take us long to find out that partisans were actually thin on the ground in Sicily. Few of the country folk and villagers could drum up any enthusiasm for the war. Their larders had been picked clean, first by the Italian army then by the Germans, and they had been left to gnaw on the bones.

When we enter a town vacated by the retreating Jerries, smiling people often pour into the street to greet us:

"Welcome! Welcome! Here...I'm shake you hand!"

"We glad...so glad you come!"

"Canadians! You know my cousin, Giuseppe, eh? He been in Montreal ten...fifteen years now."

And "We wait...wait...what take you so long?"

Old people embarrass us by kissing our hands. Women sob with relief. We munch big chunks of brown Italian bread, drink sour red wine offered generously from hidden stashes, and try to explain with gestures that Montreal is a long way from Toronto.

We usually march all day and fight at night, and there are rarely big battles...more often skirmishes with a few casualties here and a few casualties there. By the time we take an objective, the Germans have often managed to pack up and move on, but once in a while we get lucky and trap someone. Taking a prisoner feels like finding the prize in a crackerjack box; it's one less guy pitching bullets and bombs at us.

Of course, we have to fit in a few hours of sleep sometime, and we try to do it when the enemy isn't in the immediate vicinity. Since it's always possible that they might be on the move and trip over us in the dark, guards are posted to watch the roads while the rest of us sleep. If anything comes near, the theory is that the guard will yell and fire his weapon to announce the visitors before they can do any damage. Unfortunately the guards are as exhausted as the rest of us, and have been known to snooze on duty. This is not encouraged. My own creative solution when I'm on guard duty is to prop my bayonet under my chin. Eyes close...head nods...chin drops...*awake again!* It's very effective. I wonder why it's not in the official procedural manual.

Oh, we made one kind of exciting bayonet charge. We were told to take a bald little hill where there wasn't much cover, so we fixed bayonets and charged on up, screaming like banshees. It was the closest thing to Hollywood glitz we've whipped up so far.

When I say 'we', don't misunderstand: as section leader, I carried a Tommy gun, not a rifle...so I *had* no bayonet. Less theatrical, no doubt, but when my belt broke half way up the hill, I was able to handle the gun with one hand, firing from the hip, and still have the other free to hold up my pants. It wouldn't have been nearly so picturesque if I'd fallen on my face, with my pants down around my ankles. Even a bayonet wouldn't have made *that* look good.

Incidentally, that firing from the hip gambit is something we try to keep in reserve for similar awkward pants-related situations. It'll make the enemy keep their heads down, maybe, but your accuracy won't be worth a damn.

Luckily, there were only a couple of machine gunners holding the top, so no more than two or three guys were hit. We took the hill. It was very dramatic. I've had more fun having teeth pulled.

That wasn't our only bayonet action. Earlier, we had attacked a location that had been an Italian officers' training depot, coming at it from the rear and charging on across the parade ground with fixed bayonets. In that case, though, we had no casualties at all. The Italian troops that were supposed to be there were all watching the bend in the road ahead so they wouldn't be surprised by ...well...*us*, I guess. When they realized the field had already been taken, they threw up their hands and gave up without a fuss.

They weren't far wrong in focusing their defence on the bend in the road, though. We've often come under terrific fire as we rounded bends in roads. It's an effective defensive strategy. The trick, though, is to defend the road the enemy's actually using.

I don't mind telling you that any bayonet charge where you don't meet any enemy at all qualifies as a great success. You just can't help being happy about it.

DODGING SHELLS

It's frustrating when a strategy fails and you can't figure out why! The Germans had been laying down an artillery barrage, and my platoon made a night attack...over stone fences...up hills. We got only so far, then came under terrific fire. It seemed to come from a bunch of machine guns firing from behind one particular stretch of rocky fence, about a hundred yards away.

We weren't going to be able to get past them head on, but I thought I had the answer. "I'll see if I can get around and flank the position." I traded my Tommy gun for the Bren gunner's weapon, and grabbed up a bag of ammo. I needed something with longer range than a submachine gun.

I led a section over, following a convenient hedge. At a break in this cover—and now at an angle from the offending enemy fire—I sprawled behind a big rock. As the German guns opened up, I set up the Bren gun on its bipod, braced it against my shoulder and blasted away. Some of the other guys in my section were firing too, but many just lay quiet. They couldn't get a good angle for a shot, and we never have ammo to waste.

I was determined to make the Jerry bastards stop!

They weren't stopping. I was really laying it on, and the stupid buggers weren't stopping! They could see where my fire was coming from, and their bullets were hitting the top of my rock cover and deflecting straight up and out, throwing off sparks and shards into the night. I would have enjoyed the spectacular show if I hadn't had to poke my head up in order to get a shot in. They were seriously pissing me off!

"Look guys…we're going to charge in and destroy those buggers. We'll show them who they're messing with!" I was sure we could do it. "They can't thumb their noses at us like this!"

"Smitty, wait!" one of my guys called out. "We're being recalled. We have to go back." He swore he had seen a recall flare go up.

I wasn't so sure. Maybe he was mistaken. I hated to abandon my heroic battle plan. But the other guys seemed eager to get back where they'd come from.

"Ok…ok," I said. "We'll give the sons of bitches a break. Is *this* ever their lucky day!"

The next morning I found out that we'd been about to attack a couple of bloody Tiger Tanks, dug into the hill behind that stone fence.

"Well," I said, as coolly as possible. "That would explain our limited success in routing them." In fact, we'd had *no* success.

Several guys in my platoon scowled, almost as if they thought I'd exposed them to unnecessary danger.

"Hey!" I reminded them. "The tanks did pull out this morning, didn't they?" But I think we all suspected it wasn't because they were worried about us attacking them. All we could have done was to sneak over and kick at them, maybe. Anything else would have been a useless waste of ammunition, and have no more effect than the teeny midges that swarm around your head in the springtime. You don't want to breathe them in, but they sure can't hurt you.

Tiger tanks are *huge*!

DODGING SHELLS

From the time we reached the mountains, it's been hot, dirty slogging. There's often little shelter along the way, and under the coating of dust kicked up from the road, the sun has burned my skin an impressive copper colour that blends right in with my freckles. And my hair has been bleached from red to rusty blonde, so I probably look a lot like a photo negative of myself...only in sepia tones.

We're always short of supplies; we're still wearing the same battered clothes we had when we landed. If they rip, we mend them. The crotch keeps ripping out of my own trousers, and I've had to sew and re-sew them the whole way through Sicily. You'd be proud of me—I'm learning a trade. Obviously, I'm not awfully good at it yet or they wouldn't keep ripping, but I'll be a skilled seamstress (seamster?) by the time I get them replaced. And if I don't get a few minutes free to work on them, well, I have to wear them ripped. We call it 'waving the flag', and everybody but the flag waver himself finds it very entertaining.

We're entitled to replacements, of course—it says so in our pay book—but there's no sense asking the quartermaster. I've tried. His answer never changes; it only gets grouchier. "We don't have any." It's not his fault. If the supply trucks reach us at all, the space will be taken up by ammunition, food and medical supplies—not clothes. I guess they figure: it's hot...go naked.

What my present outfit lacks in style, it makes up in creative flair. I'm wearing short pants ventilated at the crotch (I'll fix them again later today), a sweaty khaki shirt, an Italian shoulder holster with a German Luger pistol, a Tommy gun and a big, ugly stiletto. The Tommy gun was actually issued to me. The other accessories were commandeered from their various reluctant owners. I didn't get their names, so I won't likely return the stuff.

Oh, and I lost my helmet somewhere along the way so I replaced it with a fascist flag, cleverly wrapped and tied to keep the sweat out of my eyes. It's not a classic look, maybe, but it adds a touch of local colour, and it keeps the sun from frying my brain.

Some of the guys go shirtless, but I don't dare. Remember the sunburn I got the summer before I came overseas? Well, I do…and I'm not eager to let it happen again if I can avoid it. One of these days they'll invent something to protect skin from the sun, but I bet they won't issue it to soldiers!

And you might think that the short pants are the best thing for this hot weather. Well, I would have thought so, too. But when you're crawling and sliding over roots and stones, it would be a great comfort to feel a layer of khaki between the ground and your knees. Am I the first person to notice this?

With all this tramping, it's the shoes and socks that go first. My own socks are about walked to shreds, and my boots are so worn that a nail was coming up well over an eighth of an inch through one sole, and driving deeper into my foot every day. It hurt like hell, but it was still better than going barefoot, so I ignored it as best I could.

We were searching a fair-sized stone house back of our lines, preparing it for use as a temporary company headquarters, when I noticed something odd about the wall beside the door.

"Hey!" I called the others. "It looks like something's been bricked up here lately." I tapped on the wall with my gun butt. "It's hollow."

Naturally we were curious. "Surely nobody's trying to *hide* something from us!"

"Naw! It must have been a mistake...they must have meant to leave a doorway. I guess they were in such a hurry, they just forgot."

"Oh, we can fix that."

So we bashed a door-sized hole in the wall, and checked out the contents.

"For Chrissake! It's a closet!"

"Who the hell would go to this much trouble to protect their clothes? Look again. There must be jewellery or something." We probably would have taken jewellery. To repay ourselves for the trouble we'd taken creating a doorway.

"I *am* looking. There's nothing! Suits, shirts, socks, some kind of fancy dancing shoes or something...shit! Let's go."

Socks! I dove into the closet, pushing the other guys aside. They didn't care. They were leaving anyway.

I stuffed my pack with all the socks I could find. *If I wear about four at a time,* I thought, *they'll cushion my foot from that damn' nail. At least, until it gets worse.*

Life was good! I would have seriously considered killing somebody to get those socks, but I'd only had to bust down a wall. I grabbed my gun and swung on out the door—and nearly bumped, face first, into the biggest goddam German I've *ever* seen, standing in the doorway! I mean...he was gigantic! Goliath couldn't have had more than an inch or two over that guy.

I froze. Imagine the indecision: should I shoot him, and maybe make him angry...or should I simply hand over my weapon, and pray that I was too insignificant for him to bother with? Before I could decide—I admit I was favouring option number two—I glimpsed friendly uniforms with weapons drawn, standing behind him.

He was a prisoner...and he was unarmed. They were bringing him in for interrogation. Oh...well.

I slid past him and headed for the latrine. My bowels were in an uproar. It must have been the excitement of finding those socks.

Don't be thinking, though, that we're in the habit of looting and pillaging. Oh, we all pick up the odd souvenir, and flashy bits of jewellery attract some guys like they attract some crows. They know it isn't right, but they just can't resist. Stuff gets broken when we're searching through homes, but that's tough...we're looking for people who might shoot us, and we're in a hurry. And if it looks like the owner may be a Nazi sympathizer? Well, I guess we're even more careless than usual.

Of course, none of this applies to wine. We hunt out wine—any kind, anywhere, any time. And if it's there, we'll take it. Always. Bottles of wine, jugs of wine, barrels of wine. If we find it, it's ours! Tradition, you know. It's a soldier thing.

Hey! The guys say the mail is finally going out. So I'll sign off now. I don't want to miss it!

Your brother,
Tommy
Pilferer, Drunkard and All-Round Scoundrel

August 8, 1943

Kath,

Well, a couple of bits of the German metal I've been dodging hit their mark. But don't worry—they can't get rid of me that easily.

We were cutting across country to make the link between the British and the American armies near Mount Etna. Our unit had started advancing over a patch of open field, when we got orders to dig in and hold our ground. As usual, Alfie and I thought we knew better.

"What the hell are we stopping for?" grumbled Alf. "Listen...there's damn little going on out here. Sounds like Jerry's nodding off." It was true. There were only a few half-hearted shells falling, here and there.

"Yeah, it's not that far..." I agreed. We were heading for the place where an eight foot wide stream cut a gap in the hill ahead. "Let's keep on going. The rest of them can catch up whenever they feel real safe." Long on sarcasm; short on common sense.

We had barely started across when I heard the shriek of Moaning Minnies. Those are the shells from bloody great six-barrel mortars that, to tell you the truth, scare the hell out of me. I ran a few yards more then flopped down, hoping if I hit the ground hard enough it'd cave in and give me some protection.

DODGING SHELLS

I hugged that dirt for a few minutes—or it may have been a few seconds—then I heard a startled yell. *Was that Alfie?* When I raised my head a bit to check on him, my helmet flew off. I felt a nasty burn on the left side of my head and then a piece of shrapnel seared into my right shoulder. All my parts seemed to be still in working order, so I scrambled up, grabbed the helmet and stumbled back to my unit, bleeding like a stuck pig from the head wound and wondering whether maybe I should have done what I was told.

A quick glance suggested that a small chunk had been taken off the top of my left ear, and a piece of shrapnel had lodged in my right shoulder. Neither was giving me too much trouble, but the ear was pouring blood all over my only shirt.

"Just slap a patch on them," I suggested. "I'm fine."

"Sorry, Smitty. You're going to have to take a trip to the hospital."

Now, the field dressing is something we always carry with us. When I go into battle, I tuck one under the webbing on my helmet, to keep it handy. It has got to be the handiest thing since toilet paper (which we never have enough of, by the way). It's a pad of absorbent cotton with gauze 'wings' several feet long…long enough to wrap around the body a couple of times and tie in place. Neat, quick, and it works for pretty much any wound I care to imagine having.

While they tied field dressings onto my wounds, the guys were trying to piece together what had happened.

"But Smitty...your new helmet! The shrapnel cut the strap clear through...on the *left* side. That was some magic shrapnel! It must have hit the helmet, then swung around your head and sliced your ear on the other side."

"Naw! It probably hit his skull then *bounced* over to his other ear. You know what a hard head Smitty is!"

"You're both wrong. Didn't you see? It knocked his helmet right off! It must have gone right through the empty place inside his head. The helmet got in the way, is all."

"Yeah, Smitty, why bother to replace the thing if you're going to treat it so bad?"

Sure, I thought. *Mock the poor wounded soldier. Very funny.*

Alfie had caught a piece of shrapnel in his leg—I guess it was his voice I heard out there—but he was still able to walk so we set out for the first aid station together.

"Hey!" I had to have the last word. "Now that we've broken ground for you guys, don't just sit there...go on up and get a bit of what we got!"

Blood was still clogged in my ear, so I couldn't hear their replies clearly...but I thought I could pick out "Fuck you!" from several sources.

We kept up a nonchalant saunter as long as we were in view, although Alfie's leg must have been hurting like hell. But once we were on our way, we decided we might as well wring as much glory out of the situation as it offered. After all, we could now claim the distinction of being 'wounded veterans' and we were wearing the blood stains to prove it!

DODGING SHELLS

First aid wiped our wounds off and patched them up a little.

When they were done, they put us in a jeep and sent us to the British military base hospital. It wasn't far.

I jumped out of the jeep. "So…" I looked around at a collection of large tents. "Is this the 'scratch' hospital, then?"

Nobody laughed. *I* thought it was funny. Some of these Brits have no sense of humour at all.

Once they'd cleaned up all the blood—there was a lot of blood—and bandaged my ear, the doctors poked around my shoulder a bit and decided to leave whatever shrapnel was hiding there right where it was. It seems to be only small bits, and they say they'll pop out on their own some day. Like a secret mobile souvenir cache.

"So…I can go back now?" I suggested, hopefully.

"Certainly not!" The medic was offended. Clearly, I'd stumbled over some protocol or other. "We'll find you a bunk and check on you later. We'll let you know when you may leave."

"But you've patched me up just great. Thanks …really! But I feel fine now."

"You can't simply come and go as you choose, young man!"

I've noticed that the British enjoy a kind of formal—some might say officious—way of conducting themselves in their official capacities. It can be very annoying, if you pay attention. I ignore it, most times.

And now we've heard that the war in Sicily is all over except for taking a broom and a great big dust pan and sweeping the last of the Germans right off the island, so the Canadian troops have been pulled out of the action. Great! The other guys are whooping it up and getting whatever other good stuff is going around, and I'm sitting here in this damned hospital!

I have a good mind to just grab my gear and get the hell out of here.

Love, from a pissed-off war hero,
Tommy

August 18, 1943

Kath,

After writing my last letter I stuck it in my pack and bolted, back to my unit. I didn't even stay to get the blood washed out of my shirt. I figured after all our hard work we were due for some rowdy celebrating—maybe a bit of good-natured looting and pillaging—something festive!

No such luck! When I caught up with my unit, there they were...marching in the village square to impress one of the bigwigs: Monty...McNaughton ...who cares? They all drop by to tell us what a really top notch job we've done over here. In order to receive their thanks all we have to do, after fighting our way through Sicily, is spend endless hours looking natty under the hot sun. Hey! You're welcome!

And they have us all training again, in preparation for the move into Italy. I feel like a real fool. I could have been resting comfortably in the hospital with Alfie. His leg wound is keeping him off his feet for a while. But instead, here I am right...left...right...left. And all I got out of the deal was...dysentery!

Within a few days I was sick as a dog. Cramping and crapping from the dysentery, blood loss, exhaustion and skimpy rations brought me down when Jerry couldn't. They gave me twelve pills to take—two at a time. That seemed pretty conservative and the dysentery was no fun at all, so I gulped them all down at once and waited. Well, it cleared up the dysentery symptoms, all right. But four days later, I had quite another problem. I won't elaborate, but I was definitely sorry I'd been so impatient with those pills.

It turns out I didn't miss much. We aren't getting any leave. None at all! We aren't even allowed *into* the damned towns and villages. But if they think they're protecting the Italian populace against evil influences, they can think again. I understand the Brits and the Yanks have stepped into the breach and are doing enough cavorting for all of us, the lucky bastards.

The Germans are off the island now. The campaign in Sicily is over. And we're marching in the bloody square. Maybe they figure they can train us to *march* over to Italy. I wouldn't be surprised.

By the way, when I was returning to my unit after being in the hospital, I stopped at a Canadian Red Cross truck to buy a candy bar. I was digging the change out of my pocket when I noticed that the package had "Free to Canadian Troops" marked clearly on the back.

"Hey!" I turned to the guy next to me. "Look at this."

He glanced at the wrapper. "Yeah...I know."

"But they're charging me for it!"

"They always do."

"So," asked the driver, "Do you want it or don't you?"

I paid for the candy and left. *Thanks for nothing.* I hope he noticed the blood on my shirt.

DODGING SHELLS

What was I up to before that shrapnel slowed me down? Well, it wasn't all just wine and socks, you know. War is serious business!

Our usual strategy is to infiltrate an area held by the Germans then hold our position, hoping that they'll pull back to avoid getting cut off from their main force. It often works, if you're stubborn enough. And that's a good thing, because our platoon doesn't have the fire power to do it any other way. There are usually more of them than there are of us, and they're *always* better equipped.

I don't know what went on when we were on our way over here, but somebody in high places must have taken a serious loss playing poker with the Brits. Because when we arrived in Sicily, we found that most of our shiny new Canadian equipment had been traded for scratty old British crap. Some of the vehicles still had sand from North Africa sloshing around in the gas tanks, for god's sake. And we're chronically short of ammunition. The Jerries, on the other hand, seem to *crap* bullets and shells.

Besides my weapons, I usually carry a small battle pack weighing about fifteen pounds or so with a rolled-up gas cape strapped to the bottom and a mess kit on the back. Emergency rations and a field dressing stashed in pouches, a water canteen, ammo holders (preferably full), and a bayonet holder are hanging off me here and there, with maybe a couple of grenades attached to battle webbing up front. The bayonet isn't used much as a weapon, but it comes in handy for digging trenches; the entrenching tool was no bloody good at all, and broke long ago. But when the shells start falling, you don't wait for fancy equipment; you *kick* a hole in the ground if you have to and hunker down in it, then dig out the most uncomfortable stones with your fingers when you have the time. Trenches aren't what they used to be, anyway. No fancy stuff—that didn't work worth a damn in the last war, and we've learned our lesson. Just find a shell crater or a hole in the ground the size of a midget's grave...and cram yourself in as best you can. Quick, temporary and scattered. Give the enemy nothing to aim at.

The mess tin has two handles that fold out for holding it over a fire. There are blocks of methyl alcohol you can light to heat stuff and a cooker stand to hold food or water. For emergency rations, we get a little brick of something that passes for meat, a block of chocolate-looking stuff with grainy bits in it and a few hard tack biscuits that could break your teeth. They can keep you going for a couple of days; you'll only *wish* you were dead.

Our usual food is pretty lousy: stringy tinned mutton...limp grey vegetables...it rarely has much flavour at all, and when it does, it tastes really bad. I guess I'm lucky; Mom was never a great cook, so I don't much notice the difference.

Uncle Ralph used to say that Mom couldn't parboil shit for a tramp. You know how Dad always stood up for her. He insisted that she *could*.

Anyway, it's worse for the other guys. They bitch about it a lot:

"What's in that can? Is that the green muck or the yellow muck?"

"It's the green muck."

"Oh. Good. The yellow muck—it's a lot worse."

DODGING SHELLS

Those were the good times—the times when our supplies actually reached us. We were moving so fast that the supply trucks often had trouble getting to us, and anyway...food doesn't get priority over ammo when space is short. So we were kind of hungry a lot of the time and really hungry some of the time.

We had run out of supplies for two or three days when we came across a peach orchard. We couldn't believe our luck. Dozens of trees, decked with ripe, juicy peaches...taunting us from behind a fence.

Well, men will do terrible things when they're not fed. I leaped that fence like it was an Olympic hurdle and stole those peaches. We all did. Not just a few peaches. We ate a *lot* of peaches. We *wolfed* down peaches. They were delicious. We ate peaches till we were stuffed and then we ate more—because they were there.

By the time I wiped the last of the peach juice off my chin, my lips were swollen up like sausages, and they stayed that way for long enough to be really embarrassing. Maybe it was a punishment for robbing the poor farmer. Probably not. But it was bloody uncomfortable, all the same, and I'll never eat another peach. Ever. Don't offer me any. I'm serious.

As we approached the Mount Etna area, our battalion was spread over the fields. At the end was a promontory where, apparently, the British Malta brigade had been positioned. We understood that we were in partial reserve, so we paid little attention when a flock of British soldiers appeared, running back through our boys. The officer who accompanied them marched smartly along, as dapper as you like, with a baton tucked neatly under his arm. His uniform was immaculate and I could have sworn I saw a shine on his boots. He had the look of an old-fashioned schoolteacher, leading a pack of rowdy schoolboys on a Saturday outing—to study butterflies, maybe. It was the damnedest thing.

"Steady on, lads…" he urged. "Steady on…" How very British. It was kind of impressive, actually.

His men appeared to be upset about something. But we couldn't hear any firing or anything, and none of them seemed eager to stop and chat, so we put it down to British eccentricity and ignored them. We'd been marching all day, and we wanted lunch.

Leaving half of the platoon picnicking in the field, our lieutenant climbed up with his batman to make sure that the empty ridge above us was secure, and he sent me with my section to guard the road ahead, where some shots had been heard.

Shit! I thought. *I'm just as hungry as the rest. No damn' wonder he's not hungry. I saw him scoffing down all the jam this morning at breakfast. The bastard ate his own portion and he helped himself to ours as well. And not for the first time, either!* He was from Toronto like the rest of us, but he was from the wealthy part of town and seemed to have been coddled all his life. It was hard to warm up to him.

The road curved around the flat-faced hill, which was about a hundred feet high and levelled off at the top. I grabbed the Bren gun and took three guys a short way along the road, where we lay down in the weedy ditch and watched for tanks. For about fifteen minutes, all I heard was my own stomach grumbling.

Suddenly, the sound of a German machine gun ripped out from the hilltop. Maybe this was more serious than we thought. Was that gun firing at *us*?

Looking up, I saw the Lieutenant and his batman stand up, clearly silhouetted against the blue sky. Their hands were raised. The enemy had gotten behind, and surprised them. A moment later, a German soldier appeared, crouching behind them with a gun, peering around. He was no fool; he had captured them and he didn't intend to be surprised in turn. I could have shot the German right then, but I didn't want to risk hitting the batman—or even the Lieutenant, I suppose. Besides, the whole goddam German army could have been back there, for all I knew.

"We're going back," I whispered. We started to slip back along the roadway a piece.

Then: "You," I turned to one of my men. "Go back to the unit and tell them...we have a problem." I left another with the Bren gun to watch the road, and led the third in a rush up to the top of the hill to see if there was anything to be done. There was nobody there. Nobody at all.

My companion was looking into two foxholes. "Here's their gear, Smitty. The Jerries must have taken them away already."

About eighty yards away, across a scruffy open field, was a stone farmhouse. We hadn't gone far enough along the road to see it before. The firing had stopped. Was anybody there?

There was no point asking for backup. We rarely have a radio available, and this was no exception. There wasn't time for one of us to go back for help.

"We have to find out if there's anything there," I said. "Cover me." I handed him my Tommy gun, and he put his rifle aside. With a Luger in one hand and a Biretta—a recent acquisition—in the other, I charged across that field to the house like I thought I was John Wayne! Too late, I remembered that John Wayne's charges were actually across a Hollywood movie set on a back lot somewhere safe in California. Probably that's why they worked out so well for him.

Now, I want you to understand exactly how stupid this was. I had no chance. Absolutely none. There was no cover, and for all I knew, that farmhouse could have been filled with dozens of Germany's best, jostling each other for a shot at any intruder. And here I was, with a pistol in each hand, pelting across the open field like an idiot—like I was daring them to mow me down. The best I could hope for would be that they might be laughing so hard they'd miss their aim and just reach out and grab me when I got close to the door.

So why did I do it? Well...we'd been sent out on a mission... we'd failed... my officer had been captured. I had to redeem *something* from this fiasco, and I simply didn't know what the hell else to do! And once I started, I figured: *in for a penny, in for a pound.* So I kept on going.

The house was empty. I could tell because I was still standing and the air was free of flying metal. I edged around to the back. A British soldier knelt with his rifle, braced against a fence post, guarding against enemy fire from the field behind. I called out to him, "How's it going, buddy? What's been happening up here?" in my best Canadian accent. I didn't want him to swing around and shoot me by mistake. He didn't even flinch.

When I came up beside him and looked in his face, I could see the neat raw bullet hole in the middle of his forehead. He was stone dead. And there was another guy just as dead as he was, leaning against the next fence-post, about sixteen feet away. They were from the Malta Brigade, and it must have been their buddies we had seen in the field below, routed by surprise enemy action.

I guess they were left behind to guard the house. And they had done it faithfully. They must have been gunned down by a small German scouting party; if it had been a bigger force, it would have stayed, in hopes of doing more damage. But the Jerries had gone, and not a moment too soon or they would have seen my witless charge across that field. And I suspect, from the evidence, that those particular Germans had no sense of humour at all, so the comic quality of my bravado wouldn't have saved me.

Now I had to go back and report this stunning example of pointless heroism to my superior officers. They listened to the whole story, then:

"Corporal, was there nothing you could have done to free the lieutenant?" It was the army. They had to ask.

"Nothing that didn't involve getting me killed." I replied. "And I even gave *that* a good try!"

I believe they might have briefly considered recommending me for a special medal—for Heroic Stupidity in the Absence of the Enemy—but there were other battles to fight, and it must have slipped through the cracks.

When I got back to my unit and the story got around, I had to face a more critical assessment.

"You might fool the officers, Smitty. But you can't fool us!"

"Yeah. You let them take the lieutenant because he ate all our *jam* again this morning. Boy, you can really hold a grudge!"

"That's ridiculous," I replied. "I hardly thought of that at all at the time."

Oh…we saw the Americans one more time. We'd made a sudden attack over the only bridge into a small town. We held the town; we held the bridge. Suddenly, we heard a roar overhead, and took cover.

"It's dive bombers! They're bombing the bridge. Shit!" The explosions rattled our teeth.

"Hey…aren't those *American* planes?"

By the time the sky was clear and we were able to come out and assess the damage, the bridge was rubble. Luckily, everyone had been able to get out of the way in time, although for the guys guarding the bridge it had been a close call.

I heard that the Americans *knew* we'd taken that town. They were very sorry. They'd been aiming at another bridge altogether, but I guess one Sicilian town looks much like another from the sky. Well, believe me, when those bombs were hitting the ground, those American planes felt exactly like German planes to us. And anyone fording the stream under that shattered bridge will agree that the damage was quite as inconvenient as if they were.

We just heard that one of our Canadian soldiers—a Chinese guy—disappeared from his unit a couple of weeks ago. There's no place a reasonable person would go AWOL here, so they searched, and finally found him up a tree. He'd tied all his belongings up in the branches, and he wouldn't come down. (I didn't see this myself, but I can picture it, with his stuff decorating the branches like some kind of drab, lunatic Christmas tree.) So they decided he was batty and shipped him home on a Section Eight.

We all had a good laugh at the poor guy's expense. But now he's home, and we're not. Who knows...maybe he's on to something.

Willing to consider all options,

Two-Gun Tommy

August 27, 1943

Dear Kath,

I see, from your last letter, that Dad and Mom haven't changed a whole lot.

Dad can whistle past just about anything and keep on smiling. And I'm not worried about Mom. She'll find a way to squeeze every drop of drama out of any situation, and no worry over me will spoil her enjoyment for long. Mom is no delicate flower.

But I'm glad you reminded her that nobody could have stopped me from enlisting. No...no need for anyone else to take the blame for that. It was all me. And, believe me, there've been moments when I've wondered why I was so damned enthusiastic about it. Patriotism? Sure...we couldn't let the Germans take over the whole bloody world, could we? And I didn't see how the Brits were going to stop them without us.

Of course, when I had to choose between going back to school and a free chance to see the world, it wasn't much of a contest! I was never able to stay out of trouble for long anyway; it was years before I realized that the school day was supposed to end at 3:30. I always stayed till 4:00 for detention... whether I was told to or not! Too much clowning around, I guess. Too many silly pranks and too much fighting. Hell, I was a redhead, living across the lane from the Columbus Boys' Club. I walked past the Italians hanging out there every day. I *had* to learn to fight.

DODGING SHELLS

Excitement... glory... the fight for freedom? Yeah, yeah. Sure. But the main reason I joined up? I was so bloody sick of hearing all the Italians on Markham Street bragging that the British were going to get their asses beaten off in Italy. I thought, "I'll show them!" And I figured that the infantry was the best place to get in on the fighting. Of course, it's also an outstanding place to get damaged. But we thought we were invincible—we didn't believe for one minute that *we* could die. Now? Well, now I'm not so sure.

When England declared war, we all knew that Canada would have to do the same before long. (We were only dragging our feet for a couple of days to show that we had a mind of our own, I guess.) So I was ready. As soon as Canada began mobilizing, I went over to the recruiting office for the 48th Highlanders with Kenny Mason. Kenny was a massive guy—used to be a truck driver. He'd been in the 48ths for a while (he was a bugler) and everybody knew him. They must have liked him a lot, because they were still kind of picky at that time, and they gave me a huge break: when I admitted I'd only turned sixteen, and weighed about 148 pounds, they didn't just kick me out on my ass. But the 48th prided themselves on taking only the fittest...and my high school football record wasn't going to cut it there.

The officer looked me over. I give him full credit—he didn't laugh. "Go home." he said. "Eat a dozen bananas, drink a quart of milk, and be eighteen by the time you get back here tomorrow."

The next day, I was back...stuffed full of bananas and milk, and prepared to lie through my teeth.

"How old are you?"

"I turned eighteen in July, sir."

The medical examiner had doubts. "Are you sure your mother knows you're here?"

"Sure she does!" I declared, without batting an eye. *If she did, she'd blow a gasket,* I thought.

They must have been able to spot a diamond, however rough, because they signed me up. While I was waiting to be sworn in, a kindly corporal in the military police tried to put me at ease.

"This way, son," he said, as though I was his younger brother. "Just stand over here. You won't have to wait long." I appreciated his concern—it was a bit scary.

As soon as I had signed on the dotted line and stepped back into the room, I stopped in the doorway and gave him a big grin. It was nice to have a friend...

"Get over there, soldier!" he bellowed. "You're blocking the way!"

I dropped the grin. I was in the army now.

Before I could think of changing my mind, they handed me a kilt left over from the First World War, a sporran (*What the hell is **that**,* I wondered), webbing and an armload of dirty equipment, and let me know I could count on $1.10 a day, free dental and medical care, and three square meals a day as long as it wasn't too inconvenient.

You'll remember that Dad cleaned up my equipment for me. I remember that I didn't even know how to *wear* the stuff properly without his help.

"You'd think they'd provide an instruction booklet or something. Do they want us to start right out making fools of ourselves?"

"Oh, probably," said Dad. "All the easier to poke fun at the raw recruits. It's tradition."

They used to exercise us on the University of Toronto campus: general physical training as well as marching, holding a rifle, falling down...how to hold a rifle while falling down (without shooting someone you liked)...and the lot of us, of course, wearing those kilts.

"The true Highlander takes a great pride in the proper wearing of the kilt, laddies," said the Drill Sergeant. "We're tough! No need to swathe the limbs in pantaloons."

"Sir?"

"What, boy?"

"Um...what are we supposed to wear...um ...*under* the kilt?"

"Under the kilt?"

"Yes, sir."

"Nothing."

"Nothing?"

"Nothing. It's tradition."

You'll believe me when I say we were dismayed. But it was tradition. Nothing.

So there we were, running across the campus with our rifles in hand and our kilts flapping around our bare knees. (I now understood the function of the sporran. It held the kilt down in front. Important.)

"Down!"

We flopped down. And the kilts flipped up. A cheer went up, and I realized that we had an audience. The university co-eds were expressing their warm appreciation of our...military skills.

We didn't dare move...and the Drill Sergeant let us lie there a while. Long enough to realize that every guy with even the slightest experience had ignored the tradition, and had his butt decently covered by standard army-issue underwear. Only the raw and impressionable recruits had been green enough to follow orders. We alone provided the entertainment for the girls, who, by now, were applauding enthusiastically. I'm sure I even heard a few complimentary comments—completely un-solicited and most unwelcome at that particular moment.

The Exhibition grounds are being used as a barracks, now, eh? When I heard we'd be billeted in the stalls at the Horse Palace until we were shipped overseas, I'll admit I was a bit insulted. I'd never paid much attention to the décor there. But have you ever really *looked* at that building? It's the most elegant place *I'd* ever slept in!

With so many new recruits, I guess they couldn't be sure that everybody would wake up promptly and full of energy in the morning, so they paraded the whole damned marching band down the aisles between the stalls, treating us to a rousing tune. It sounded like thunder and light-ning...only louder. A *lot* louder. I admire the man who could sleep through that. None of *us* did!

DODGING SHELLS

The first morning, they herded us into the ring, where temporary troughs had been installed, with running water for washing up. We splashed ourselves awake and then we were lined up for inspection.

"Okay," snapped the officer. "You're a sorry enough looking bunch. Did you all shave?"

"Yes sir!" Many voices.

I said nothing.

He stopped right in front of me. Of course.

Suspiciously: "Soldier! Did you shave this morning?"

"No sir."

"Why not?"

"I didn't need a shave, sir." I'd never shaved in my life.

"From now on, you shave. Every morning."

"Yes sir!"

And I did. Every morning. It didn't take long. I never put a blade in the razor.

I expect they'll start up the Exhibition again as soon as the war's over, but I don't think I'll ever be able to enjoy the Pure Food Building the same way again. We used it as our mess hall, and it's the first place I encountered kippers. They were canned …they were dry…and they were left over from the First World War! Apparently, the British consider them a food source. It lowered my expectations for our stay in England; I hoped it would be a short one.

Just before we were shipped overseas, we sustained a terrible blow. We were issued new battle dress, you remember. The government wanted all the troops to be dressed alike—a glorious united Canadian army. We had to turn in our kilts. Yes...the perfectly tailored work of art you'd altered so carefully for me...gone. I tried to shield you from the grief, but I think enough time has gone by...

Don't think we gave them up willingly. In fact, the dirty deed was done in the most cowardly way, one unit at a time—to prevent a mass riot!

I'm sorry.

I have plenty of time to reminisce right now. We're still in camp, trying to keep fit until we're shipped out. I suppose I should try to appreciate the break, but they haven't laid on much in the way of entertainment during the wait, so it's kind of tedious.

Once we're on the move, I don't know when I'll be able to write. Be sure to take care of your-self...and I'll try to do the same.

Rested and waiting,
Tommy

October 2, 1943

Kath,

I haven't had much time to write, because we're moving fast.

By the time they piled us into trucks and dropped us on the beach at the Straits of Messina, we were ready to take on both the Germans and the Italians on the mainland—a bit grimmer than we'd been before the Sicily landing, maybe, but ready. We didn't know what to expect, so we steeled ourselves to meet whatever might come. Nothing was going to catch us by surprise. That's what we thought.

They loaded us onto an LCT (*Landing Craft, Tank*, that is) and we knew we weren't going to be first on the beach this time. The main resistance would be absorbed by the guys going in before us, and we were to fight our way past them.

The landing was a lot quieter than we had expected—no real resistance—but we figured we had hit a lucky patch and immediately started marching north and east, up the 'foot' of Italy...watching around every bend in the road and ready for anything. As we neared one town, a swarm of Italian soldiers poured over the hill toward us...on the run.

We stopped cold.

"What the hell! They said this town had already been taken!"

"Shit! There must be thousands of them!"

"Nah…hundreds maybe…"

"That's plenty!"

We hadn't expected *this*. They'd sent us out here to face the entire goddam Italian army! We aimed our weapons.

"Wait…something's wrong."

"You're bloody *right* something's wrong!"

"No…they're, um, jogging or something. They're not aiming their weapons. I don't think they want to fight…"

Apparently that jog was the Italian parade quick-march. Those soldiers were coming to formally surrender, and they had made a little spectacle of it. We were kind of glad we hadn't shot any of them. *That* would have been embarrassing.

They weren't the only ones. As we marched through the villages, we came across plenty of Italian soldiers waiting, with their kits laid out neatly for inspection, ready to surrender. We thought we were prepared for anything, but this really took the cake. I'll say this for them…they were sure tidy.

Of course, not all of the Italian soldiers were so co-operative. Occasionally a pocket of tougher troops dug in and there'd be a skirmish. We never knew quite what to expect. But as we marched north, we constantly passed Italian soldiers heading south to surrender. I couldn't help thinking about those mouthy Italian guys who gave me such a hard time back home, bragging that the British were going to get their asses beaten off by Mussolini's finest. They were so damn' cocky when the war started…I wonder what they've been up to all this time? Besides shooting hoops in the park, I mean.

Within a few days, we heard that Italy had surrendered to the Allies. Now we only have one army to fight. But it's a doozie!

We still haven't received a lot of our heavy equipment, so we have to make do with that dilapidated British stuff. Some of the trucks don't even have brakes. I've seen them being towed along, each chained to two other vehicles—one in front to pull it up each hill, and one in back to stop it from careening down the other side. All civilian vehicles are fair game for expropriation, of course, and there are probably some Italian troop trucks in the mix as well. We ride when we can, steal bicycles when we find them, and march when nothing else is available. But we'd been trained to walk-and-run twenty or thirty miles at a stretch, wearing twenty-five pound packs. So we were moving right along.

I've heard that travel helps you appreciate other cultures. I wonder if the people who say so are really keeping their eyes open. Late one afternoon, we stopped to rest near one of the villages scattered along the way. It had been a pretty easy march—no resistance to speak of—but we'd been moving fast all day and we were bushed. We lounged in a small slice of shade, using the sides of a huge round vat as a backrest, and watched as quaint peasants tipped in baskets full of plump purple grapes. It was a perfect Italy moment.

"Look…they must be making wine!"

"Push your gear out of their way. There can *never* be too much wine."

The vat had a wooden floor, with a giant wooden screw in the centre to press the juice out of the grapes.

"What the hell is that mule doing in the bloody vat?"

"The screw can't turn by itself, can it? The mule's attached to that beam thing, and that turns the screw. He just keeps trudging around in there..."

"That's disgusting. He's tromping on those grapes with his big, dirty feet!"

"That's nothing...didn't you see? He pissed on the grapes!"

"Wait...how long does he stay in the vat?"

"All day, I guess."

"All day."

"Yeah."

"Well...sooner or later that mule is going to have to take a dump."

Geez. It could almost take away your appetite for the wine altogether!

Part way up the toe of Italy, we veered off into the mountains to do some reconnaissance. We would be continuing along the coast, and the last thing we needed was an enemy force on the heights, firing down on us like we were fish in a barrel.

The Germans are retreating as we head north, but they do what they can to make us feel unwelcome. Naturally, it was when my platoon was out a couple of hours in advance of the battalion, searching for any tell-tale signs of resistance, that they spotted us trotting along the road. They must have been pissed off that we were following so close on their heels, because they promptly started shelling the hell out of us.

A few dozen yards ahead, there was a small stone bridge that looked like it had been there since the beginning of time. We figured a few shell hits more or less wouldn't finish it, so we climbed under and lit up our smokes. I guess it must have looked good to the civilian population, too, because we were soon joined by a couple of shrieking women with about seven bawling kids in tow. They were followed by a number of aunts, a large handful of uncles and somebody's grandmother...all huddled under there, screaming and wailing like their asses were on fire. Their caterwauling was so deafening, echoing in that damned tomb, that we couldn't stand it; one by one, we crawled out over the crowd to sit on the bank in the shell fire. We preferred to take our chances with the Jerries.

"I'd better go back and get help," I offered, un-enthusiastically.

Nobody objected. "We'll be here." Sure. Where were they going to go?

I certainly wasn't going back along the road—that would have been suicidal—so I took off over the hill under some mean shell fire. Since we weren't visible on the road any more, the Germans were scattering shells all over the place, in hopes of scoring a hit. It was rough going, through trees and bush, but eventually I got around to the road behind and trudged back toward the battalion. By the time I reached them, I was exhausted.

I reported to the officer. "You've got to watch out, about three turns up front. The Jerries are up there, shelling my guys. They're pinned down." It was a mountain road. It twisted and turned like a Christmas tree garland.

"Are they watching the road?"

"You're goddam right they are!"

"How did you get back?"

"I kept to the hills." It sounded rugged, dramatic. I tried to look nonchalant, but it wasn't easy. I was sweating like a pig.

"Can you get us back up there?"

My spirits fell. I was really tired. But I couldn't spoil the moment.

"Yeah," I said. "Sure."

So I led the whole battalion back along that road, until I spotted the hill I was looking for.

"This is it."

It was tough going. The rest of the battalion was more heavily armed than I was. But I led them over.

The wrong hill.

Maybe it was the fatigue. One hill looked a lot like another. Anyway…there was nobody there. Nobody.

A lot of sweaty men glared at me. Several muttered, ominously.

"I guess it's the next hill," I admitted, you can't imagine how reluctantly. "Sorry."

Another medal—I could almost feel it—snatched away by the prankish fingers of fate.

The officer looked at me. "I think we'd better just keep going along the road," he said, without further comment. I felt like a complete ass. I had led the whole battalion over a mountain…for nothing.

DODGING SHELLS

You'd think it couldn't get worse, wouldn't you? Well, by the time the battalion followed the road around the hill and reached my men, the Germans had pulled back. They were gone. So were the terrified civilians. My men were lounging by the side of the road enjoying a smoke.

This did not make me look better.

When we got back to the coast, we were moving fast, walking as often as we rode and carrying the weapons we need to fight the enemy up close. Along one stretch, where the road ran alongside a crumbling stone wall, something flew over the wall and hit one of the guys in the head. He swung around in a crouch, grabbing for his rifle.

"What the fuck was *that*?"

A ripe, red tomato rolled to a stop in the road.

"Who the hell *did* that…do you see anybody?" We didn't.

Then a small face, none too clean, appeared over the wall, attached to a scrawny body and wearing a few rags and a big grin. He lobbed over another fat tomato. This one was aimed at me. I caught it with my free hand and sunk my teeth into it.

"This is great, kid. Shoot some more over!"

"That kid has a great arm…maybe we should take him with us. He'd come in handy pitching grenades at Jerry!"

Before long, there were half a dozen Italian urchins perched on the wall and firing tomatoes at us as we marched by. And as fast as they came, we caught them and wolfed them down. We took a few hits, but it was worth it. Fresh, juicy tomatoes. It was a vegetable buffet!

You see, our menu had been leaning heavily on canned bully beef and cheese sandwiches at the time...not inedible, but boring as hell.

"Listen, guys," suggested Zeke, one afternoon, "why don't I take half of this bully beef and trade it for some tomatoes. Maybe there's an Italian farmer out there who has too many tomatoes and doesn't know how bad this stuff tastes. My mother used to make a great stew with beef and tomatoes." Zeke is the only Mohawk Indian in our troop; for that matter, he's the only Mohawk I've ever met.

We didn't need to think twice. Fresh stew! We loaded Zeke up with cans of bully beef and waited for dinner to arrive. We waited a long time.

Finally, Zeke staggered back into camp.

"Zeke...buddy...are you okay? What happened?"

Zeke grinned a foolish, sleepy grin. "M'fine. Jus' need t'sleep."

"He's drunk! Zeke...where are the tomatoes?"

"Tomatoes?" His eyelids drooped stupidly.

"Look in his knapsack. Where's his knapsack?"

"Here it is...it's empty."

"Shit! He traded the beef for wine!"

"Well...so where's the wine? Zeke, where the hell's the wine?"

Zeke looked confused. Then he brightened up. "S'okay. I *drank* the wine."

Our dinner was gone, and he'd *drunk* all the wine. "You sonofabitch!" I squawked. I grabbed him by the throat and tried to squeeze the life out of him. "You rotten pig sonofabitch!"

The guys tried to pull me off him, half-heartedly—they were pretty mad too—but I was past reasoning. All I could think about was that stew. Even stupid drunk, Zeke knew he was in serious trouble. His bladder, full of all that wine, gave way and he pissed himself.

"That's enough!" I wasn't so crazy that I'd ignore the Sergeant's voice. Zeke had come close to passing out. I let him go.

It was a while before he could breathe freely enough to speak. He glared at me, eyes all bloodshot, and snarled, 'I'm gonna kill you!"

I ignored him. He was drunk.

But when I went to bed that night, I decided to take the side of the tent where Joe usually slept. (Joe was my tent-mate.) I was hungry and I wasn't thinking too clearly...but in the back of my mind, I figured:

Zeke probably won't do a damn' thing...but if he does, it'll be tonight. This way, if he tries to knife me, he'll get Joe, instead and I'll have time to jump him. Boy, he'll be sorry! I'll get him good...there's no way I'll let him get away with it. Joe's my pal!

I'm not sure Joe would have been real happy with my solution...but it made sense to me at the time, and I didn't think to check with him. I slept like a log, and I guess Zeke did too. The next morning, he didn't remember a thing.

One of the most common souvenirs we brought out of Sicily, because it's so darned portable, is malaria. It wasn't enough for the mosquitoes to torment us—they had to leave us with a lasting reminder: headache, fever, vomiting, chills and random bouts of hallucination. Every day, the officers make sure that each soldier takes his nepadrine pill. If scary yellow pee suits your fancy, nepadrine is definitely the stuff you want. Unfortunately, it isn't always effective against the disease. It didn't protect me. I didn't have to be hospitalized for it like some of the guys, but they say the symptoms can recur, even years later. Great. There's nothing like a cold sweat to bring back fond memories.

They've started to call us Monty's Mountain Goats. Before we got to the east coast, we swung back into the mountains, where we started to meet German rear guard action again. And to make things worse, within a few days it started to snow, with occasional sleet as a change of pace. Not a lot of snow by Canadian standards, but snow, all the same. How is this a problem, you ask? Well, remember the snappy outfit I was wearing in the hot Sicilian sun...with the shorts and all? I'm still wearing that. And it's bloody cold. You see, it's only early October, and the British rules don't allow for changing into long pants until—oh, I don't know—some damn time *after* early October.

But I guess it doesn't really matter, because we have nothing else to change into anyway. Warmer clothing hasn't reached us yet. The drivers from company headquarters and the motorcyclists have leather jerkins, and sometimes they fashion sleeves out of blankets to make a sort of jacket. But *we're* lucky if we get food. The farther north we move, the farther our supplies have to be trucked, and over bad roads all the way. From the trucks, we haul the stuff to the front lines on our backs, so we're unlikely to be hauling luxuries. Apparently adequate clothing qualifies as a luxury. We keep moving during the day and curl up under a rubber gas cape at night and hope we don't freeze in our sleep.

The Germans use these mountains as natural fortresses, defending them one by one as they pull back northward, blowing up bridges and mining roads behind them as they go. We can come across them anywhere. That wouldn't be such a problem if we had as much ammunition to waste as they have. But we don't. So here's what we do: the guys up front advance, firing into an area, and go right on past. If there are any Jerries there, this is sure to catch their attention, and they'll start shooting. It's an automatic response...like slapping at mosquitoes. The troops coming up behind watch to see where the firing's coming from, and try to pick off the shooters before they're able to mow down those first guys. It's efficient and it's economical, but nobody much wants to be one of those fellows out in front.

When we do come across them, the Germans are almost always dug in and firing from behind cover. We rarely actually see them unless we trip over their dead or wounded on our way by. But when we do take prisoners, we want to hold on to them. They, on the other hand, tend to want to leave. So you can see how tension could develop. Any wrong move on the part of a prisoner—a look, an attitude—might mean he's about to start trouble or try to break loose or something, and we don't want to have to waste ammunition on him a second time. Usually a quick belt in the mouth with a rifle butt will cool things down. It's brutal, but war's not for sissies.

It's much too easy to get careless over here. We're liable to get shelled at any time, so you kind of get used to it. Our sergeant—we call him Rusty (he's a redhead like me, only older)—was one of those happy-go-lucky Irish guys who's great company in a bar room. He never took anything seriously. Rusty would trot through a hail of shell fire like it was a shower of confetti.

One day we had been out on patrol, clambering over the hills till we were hotter and sweatier than usual. Rusty plopped down on a hillside to rest for a few minutes, with his helmet under his head and his legs sprawled out...as easy as if he was sunning in the park. Suddenly, a barrage of shellfire rained down on us from a copse of trees that was way too close for comfort. We should have checked.

We all dove for cover, except Rusty. He had jackknifed bolt upright...and he just sat there.

"Rusty...what's up? Get over here! Hey, are you alright?"

Rusty looked at us. He didn't move. "A shell fell."

"Yeah. Were you hit?"

"I dunno."

"Well, for Chrissake...where did it fall?"

"Between my legs. It fell between my legs."

"Shit! Are you okay?"

"I dunno." Rusty was afraid to look.

A small shell had torn the crotch right out of his pants, but it missed all the private bits. Rusty was fine, but he's a changed man. His careless days are over. He watches for Germans everywhere. *Everybody* wants to go on patrol with Rusty.

Pushing through these mountains, Alf and I seem to do more than our share of scout patrol. (Alf re-joined us before we crossed to Italy and his leg is pretty much healed by now.) Someone has to find out what Jerry's doing, to avoid awkward surprises. We check out the ground the others plan to travel and sneak craftily up on any enemies we find, in order to learn just how much trouble they are likely to give us. Then we report the news back to our officers. Ideally, the Germans never know we've been there. We take care that they won't. Otherwise, they shoot at us. And we'd rather they didn't.

But it doesn't always work out so smoothly. We were out on patrol a couple of weeks ago with our buddy Bill, checking for Jerries on the other side of a wooded hill. We stripped down to the minimum possible equipment, and definitely nothing noisy. We crept through the underbrush, using hand signals to communicate, and didn't make a sound. We did everything right. But when we reached the top, we found ourselves practically face to face with a small German patrol. They were as shocked as we were. They fired. We fired. They ran.

"They're gone," I said, "Everybody ok?" No reason to keep quiet now!

"No." Bill's face was ashy white. "They got me in the leg." His pants were soaked with blood.

I pulled out a field dressing and we tied it tight enough to stop the bleeding. No bones were broken. Bill was the toughest one of us all. He'd be ok.

"Hang on, buddy. We'll get you back alright."

He nodded, silently.

We wrestled him back down the hill, and started back to our unit. Half way there, Bill went limp.

"He's out cold," Alf noted. "We'll have to carry him."

"Good." I said. "Poor bastard. That must have hurt like hell."

It couldn't have been more than fifteen minutes before we reached our unit.

We eased Bill to the ground, and a captain who had seen us struggle in knelt down beside him. He didn't call for a medic or transportation. *Why wasn't he calling for a medic or transportation?*

"I'm sorry, fellows. He's gone."

No. He couldn't be. The wound…it had been no big deal! No broken bones, and we'd pretty well stopped the bleeding. Bill was a rugged guy.

He had died of shock.

We were stunned. There had been practically nothing wrong with him—he had just died.

The Jerries had killed him.

The Jerries.

Alf seemed to recover first. He called me aside.

"C'mon, Smitty," he said, grimly. "We're gonna get them."

I knew who he meant. I grabbed my Tommy gun. We headed out to hunt Germans.

I don't know how long we were out. We scoured the area; it must have been hours. But they had pulled out. We didn't find anybody. Eventually, we had to go back. It was getting late.

We met our lieutenant on our way back into camp. Everyone was wolfing down rations.

DODGING SHELLS

"Where the hell have you boys been?" he barked.

"Looking for Jerry."

"Who sent you out?"

"They shot Bill. Bill's dead. We're going to keep looking till we find them and we're going to kill every last one of the bastards."

"Look, you two—quit playing the fools! You're only going to get yourselves killed…and you'll put us *all* in danger. Go eat!" But he looked like he would have joined us if he could.

We ate and slept and the next day the platoon moved on.

We never get leave. We're moving too fast. But occasionally we hear of a farmer or a townsman along the way who has a supply of some kind of alcoholic beverage (any kind will do) and is not too shy to share it with thirsty Canadian liberators—at a price, of course. An opportunity of this kind came to our attention a couple of days later, at a farmhouse near the crossroads about a mile up the road from where we had camped. Since we weren't moving out immediately, Alf and I, with a few others, hiked on up the road. The report was right, the farmhouse was cozy, and I got very, *very* drunk. By the time we had to settle up with the farmer and return, I wasn't thinking too clearly.

"Okay, paysan, how much do I owe you?" I slurred, with my arm draped in a comradely way around the shoulder of our obliging host.

The wily farmer sized up the situation, and decided that he'd met his mark for the day. He demanded his price.

"What'cha think? Ya think I'm drunk?" I was offended. "That's too gaddam much! I thought we were pals. If it wasn't for us this place would be crawling with fat, greedy Germans (instead, I guess, of thin, drunken Canadians). You're just takin' advantage!" It had been known to happen.

The farmer held his ground, and I threw a fistful of money on the table.

"Hey…wha's that over in the corner?" It was a huge crockery jug.

"Brandy," answered the farmer, hopefully. "You want some?"

I swung the jug up onto my shoulder, and strode out the door. At least, I think I strode. It's hard to judge, when you're that drunk.

"You gotta pay!" squeaked the farmer, following me out. "You gotta pay!"

"Fuck you!" I spat, quite clearly. "Bloody ingrate," I muttered, "Nothin' worse than an ingrate…"

I staggered on down the road with my buddies, carrying that mammoth jug—there must have been over three gallons of brandy in there, and the sloshing didn't help to balance the thing.

"Any of you guys gonna help me carry this?" I ventured.

"Hell, no!" they laughed. Even Alf. "You took it …*you* carry it!" This didn't improve my mood any.

About half way back to base, we were overtaken by two distinguished members of the caribonieri. (That's the Italian police.) They were armed with guns fixed with small bayonets. Probably the farmer sent them.

"Halt!" they said. And a bunch of other stuff, in Italian.

We didn't understand a word of it, but they circled around us and stood in the road blocking our way. They had their eyes fixed on the clearly visible jug on my shoulder, so we got the point.

I was getting plenty tired by then. I was still mad, and I wasn't one bit less drunk than I was when I left the farmhouse.

"Get the fuck out of my way," I snarled, "or I'm gonna shove that bayonet right up your ass!"

It's surprising how quickly you can get the drift of another language when there's a pressing need. I'm sure those cops knew exactly what I was offering.

Surprisingly…they left!

In retrospect, I imagine their thinking went something like this:

If he puts that bottle down, it looks like he might try to do just what he says. We'll have to shoot him…and we signed an armistice with these lunatics! If we shoot him right now…he drops the jug…the jug breaks…and we still have a dead Canadian on our hands.

Shit! Leave him alone. Giuseppe will have to make up the loss off the next batch of suckers that come through.

By the time I finally got near camp, I was alone. The others had gone on ahead. No wonder! They weren't hauling a giant jug of brandy. I eased it to the ground and looked at it for a moment.

What the hell do I want this thing for? I wondered. *They're never going to let me keep this.*

I left it there, in the road, and trudged on toward my tent.

I didn't bother to look for it in the morning. I knew I'd seen the last of it.

I've pieced this last episode together for you from what the other guys told me. I don't actually remember much of it, for some reason.

I don't know when I'll be able to mail this, but I'll keep it in my pack for you in the meantime. Gotta go now...we're moving forward.

Your brother,

Tommy the Unrepentant

October 10, 1943

Kath,

I've gone and done it again. I know you're going to be mad.

I'm in the hospital in North Africa, catching a little R&R and recovering from a bullet wound, but when I tell you how it happened, you'll see that I wasn't just being careless. (That's what you were thinking—don't bother to deny it.)

The Germans were causing us a lot of trouble near a key Italian town. Joe and I were struggling up a steep hill, and the rest of the platoon were following, with our tanks still circling around on our left from the other side of the hill. I had my Tommy gun and Joe was carrying the Bren gun, but he was having trouble keeping up.

I've mentioned Joe. His folks own a diner in the east end, so he never stops bitching about the food here. But Joe's a good guy. He usually comes along with Alf and me when we're off raising hell, and he knows about a million jokes. Some of them are funny even when we're sober.

"Here, Joe...gimme the Bren gun..." I offered, in order to give him a break.

"The bitch is heavy," Joe panted.

"Yeah, take the Tommy gun...it'll be easier..."

"Thanks."

We traded weapons, and I shouldered the heavier gun. Joe fell behind anyway, so I was alone by the time I neared the top of the hill. I spotted three Germans about a hundred yards ahead, right at the summit, aiming an anti-tank gun at our tanks. I had managed to come up behind them, and their attention was still focused down the slope. They weren't looking in my direction.

Behind to the left of me, I heard our lieutenant say, "It's Eby's platoon!"

Who's Eby? I thought. *Who cares...it's* **not***!*

I glanced back and there he was, with his batman nearby. To my horror, he began waving...to 'Eby' and his platoon.

I looked ahead again. I really *wanted* it to be Eby...

Nope. It was still Germans. And I didn't dare yell a warning. They hadn't noticed us yet.

Well, I thought, *at least I have the drop on them. I can take out two for sure—maybe all three. That'll slow them down a bit.*

I drew a bead on the Jerries and fired. Nothing. The gun wasn't cocked. Shit!

I cocked the gun and fired again. Again... nothing!

The bloody safety was on! Joe had given me the goddam gun un-cocked and with the safety on! *The bastard! He must have done it on purpose!* (I knew he hadn't.) *The sonofabitch wants me dead! What did I ever do to him?*

I hated Joe at that moment, with a deadly hate.

Precious seconds had been lost, and by now, the Germans had spotted me—attracted by the lunatic waving of the lieutenant, no doubt. They scooted back over the crest of the hill and started firing at us.

DODGING SHELLS

Where was Joe? Don't ask. I didn't know. I didn't care.

I was right out in the open there. No cover at all. I flipped the safety off and started to fire back, but I had to make every bullet count. I was carrying a couple of spare canisters of .45 ammo—for the Tommy gun! The Bren gun took .303. Unless that ammunition had magically transformed itself while I wasn't looking, I was going to run out of bullets, and soon. I prayed for some support. Anything at all would have been welcome!

I glanced to my left again and noticed that the lieutenant had disappeared. But his batman was still there. He'd been shot—I could see blood and bubbles seeping out of his back—and he was laying there in full sight of the Germans. I had no cover either, but I crouched behind a sorry-looking piece of scrub brush, and pretended to think it would hide me. It wasn't much, but it was better than what he had.

"Try to get closer," I encouraged the batman, "so I can pull you over here with me." At least *I* could still fire a gun…and I'd try to drag him back to safety.

I could hear my platoon moving up behind, firing at the Jerries in front of me. Oh, great! I was between them and the enemy! In desperation, I cautiously raised my left arm and waved it in the air, hoping they'd realize I wasn't just another German soldier. What were the chances that they'd recognize that arm? Well, not great, I guess. But I didn't have a whole lot of more reliable options open to me at that point.

Something that felt like a flying golf ball smashed into my shoulder. *A golf ball? What the...?* How fast had that thing been going? It *burned!* I glanced down. There was no golf ball but blood was spreading over my shirt front.

The Germans, always with an eye to the main chance, had taken the opportunity to shoot at that flailing arm, and they'd got me in the shoulder.

By now I'd run out of ammunition, and worried about my arm stiffening up before I could crawl out of there. I glanced at the batman, but the bubbles had stopped. He was dead. It was time to go. I grabbed the Bren gun and backed away, looking for a way out. The gun didn't budge. I gave it a tug with my good hand. Nope. It was caught on some roots or something. Shit! I had to leave it behind. As if this day wasn't already crappy enough! I scuttled back around the corner of a low ridge to the right of me and found my platoon, wisely screened by now from German view.

"Smitty...they got you! Let's see. How bad is it?"

"How the hell do I know? It hurts. Just patch it up. I can still move it...maybe the bone is ok..."

While they were tying on a field dressing, the lieutenant came over and asked about his batman.

"He's dead. Sorry. I couldn't help him."

He paled and turned away. I think they'd grown to be friends. "Go on to the back of the line and we'll have someone pick you up," he said. "Thanks, Smitty."

I didn't have to be told twice. I went to the back of the line and found a nice spot behind a few big rocks. I had wedged myself among them and settled in as comfortably as my shoulder would allow before I realized that there could be a problem. If the Germans took a whim to come around the other side of that ridge—the right side—I'd be out in the open! The way things had been going for me that day, it was pretty much a sure thing. *Shit!*

My shoulder was hurting like hell, and I wasn't about to move right away. I lay real still. *If they see me,* I thought, *maybe they'll think I'm dead.*

That wasn't good enough. *Do I look dead?* I wondered. *Not with **my** luck.* I inched my good arm out at an awkward angle, and tried to imagine the effect. Better. I closed my eyes, and lay still, doing my very best rendition of dead.

When I heard my platoon withdrawing past me, I miraculously 'revived'…before they got the full effect of my little tableau. I definitely didn't want them to leave me behind. An officer stopped beside me.

"We're getting out of here. Smitty…can you walk?"

"Walk?" I declared, "Hell…watch me run!"

The officer was all concern. "Look, Smitty," he said, kindly, "You go ahead. We won't go any faster than you can manage."

Oh, great! I thought. *So if the lead guy hits trouble, no big loss. I'm damaged goods anyway! Sacrifice the poor wounded guy…why not?* My shoulder was aching, and I wasn't feeling very charitable.

I decided to salvage a little something from this fiasco. "Good idea. Thanks. But you'd better send somebody out in front with me, in case I need help."

"Oh, sure! Who do you want?"

"I'll take *Joe*. Here…Joe! You'd better keep right up front here with me!"

I wasn't done hating Joe yet.

We couldn't return the way we had come—it was way too open—so we had to take the long way back, across a no-man's-land of broken countryside. When darkness fell, we still hadn't gotten back as far as the front lines, so we stopped and settled in for the night. One of the guys dug a can of condensed milk out of his pack.

"Here, Smitty," he said. "I've been carrying this long enough…you have it."

"Yeah." I heard other voices in the dark. "Give it to Smitty. You drink it, Smitty."

I knew I must look pretty rocky. They didn't even pretend to haggle over it. What a great bunch of guys! I drank the milk.

"Hey…any extra gas capes?" asked the sergeant. "It's bloody cold out here, and it's gonna get colder. We have to keep him warm."

They tucked a couple of gas capes around me.

"That's not good enough; he could go into shock. You two guys…throw your capes on the pile and crawl under there with him." I was trying not to shiver, but maybe they noticed.

It wasn't the best night's sleep I've ever had; with a man on either side of me, every time any of us shifted at all it jarred my shoulder and hurt like hell. But I was grateful for the warmth, and the shivering stopped. I didn't freeze and I didn't go into shock and in the morning I was able to keep walking.

DODGING SHELLS

We didn't have far to go. Before we reached company headquarters, we caught the rich, bracing odour of coffee. I stopped long enough for a cup, steaming hot, before I set out to trudge another mile or so to the road. Field coffee brewed in a bucket doesn't sound like much but when it's all you've got, it can taste pretty damn' good. And it was hot. I can't say enough about hot.

I'd barely reached the road before a jeep stopped.

"Hey," someone called out, "here's another stretcher case!"

"Naw," I heard myself say, "I'll be fine. I don't need a stretcher."

"When did *that* happen?" The driver nodded toward my shoulder.

"Early yesterday. Then I walked back to headquarters. I just had a coffee…don't bother about me. I can walk some more." *Shut up!* I told myself.

"Stretcher case!" He shouted. "Sit down and wait for the stretcher." *Fool,* I heard him thinking.

What the hell was I arguing about? I'd done my bit. So I decided to take any aid they were prepared to dish out. I flopped down by the side of the road, and by the time the stretcher bearers got over there to collect me, I had arranged myself to look as pathetic as they could have wanted.

The field hospital wasn't really much of a hospital at all. The doctors worked in a bunch of tents and the ground outside was littered with men on stretchers, waiting to be treated. I didn't even pretend to be urgent, so I was left to wait.

Eventually they began to distribute dinner to the stretcher cases. It was taking a while. "What's that smell?" I asked the guy next to me.

"It's macaroni."

"Macaroni...wow! Have I died and gone to heaven?"

"Don't get excited. They're serving it over there." He pointed. "It's for the walking wounded and the Italian stretcher-bearers. We get the usual crap."

It took me about fifteen seconds to get up off that stretcher and into the macaroni line. Five minutes to wolf down the pasta, and I was back on the stretcher by the time dinner arrived. The guy was right...it was crap, but it was food, and I ate it anyway. War makes animals of us all.

Eventually, they carried me into a tent, and one of the British surgeons stopped by to have a look.

"What seems to be the problem, son?"

I held up my right hand. "It's my finger," I said. "I think I've got an infection in my finger." I had. It had gotten badly infected, in fact—I don't know how—and it was hurting like hell right then.

"Your finger." He smiled, just a little. (British, you know.) "Anything else?" I guess the blood on my shirt had tipped him off.

"Oh...and I got shot in the shoulder." I grinned.

"I see. Well, let's fix you up, then." He dug the bullet out and bandaged the wound. "You're lucky." I didn't feel all that lucky. "The bullet missed the bone." Okay—now I felt lucky.

Then he cleaned and disinfected my finger and put a bloody great cast on my hand. I still don't know if it was actually necessary to immobilize the finger or if he was simply going along with the joke.

Or maybe he thought it would distract me from the shoulder wound. But whatever he did under that cast worked. It drew out the infection—you'll notice that I generously omit the disgusting description of the results—and within a couple of days, the finger was on the mend.

The next day, they loaded me onto a truck headed for the plane to Sicily. On the stretcher beside me was a wounded German officer from the elite 90th Paratroopers. He was a big, clean-cut guy wearing a well-cared-for uniform. (I, on the other hand, was still bloody and my 'ensemble' was a sorry joke.) He looked pretty fit, but I guess he'd been badly wounded.

"Hello, Canada," he said. "It seems they are kindly shipping us to a more comfortable hospital. How are you?"

"I'm fine. How about you?" Sounded like he could speak English better than I could!

"Better than I could have expected," he admitted. "They have done their best."

He seemed like a nice enough guy. We chatted to pass the time.

"You know," he smiled, "we give you Canadians special attention. We rush to our mortars when we see the red shoulder patches coming. Other troops …the sensible troops…take shelter when the mortars fire right on top of them. But you Red Patches keep running through fire. You're devils. You just keep on coming."

"Sorry," I grinned.

"I don't think you are," he responded. "You know, I've been fighting for a long time, now, and I really don't know what this is all about. Why are you and I fighting each other? We should both be fighting together."

"Fighting who?"

"Why—fighting the Russians, of course!"

I hope he recovers all right. As long as they keep him locked up tight till we're done fighting Germans.

At the hospital in Sicily, they changed my bandages and took the ridiculous cast off my hand. Once I could manoeuvre more comfortably, I was eager to wash off the stale blood and sweat. You'd think that would be a simple request, wouldn't you? Not that they weren't eager to help....

I flagged down the prettiest nurse (well, why not?) and fell right into their evil trap.

"Nurse...I'd like to clean up a bit," I said, with my most charming and boyish grin.

"Oh, of *course*," she said, smiling ever so sweetly. "Can someone help me over here with a sponge bath?"

She was joined by another nurse who was just as pretty as the first one.

"If you could point me to the shower..." I suggested.

"Oh, no! You can't get these fresh bandages wet!"

I could see the sense in that. They started to sponge the dried blood off my chest and arms so gently...it was hard not to be grateful. I closed my eyes and enjoyed the luxury of it. *Boy,* I thought, *this is the life!* By the time they started bathing the dust off my legs and feet, I had decided that I could definitely get used to this.

"Alright, now lift up." My eyes flew open. The first nurse was fumbling with my pants.

"What?" I squeaked.

"Lift up. We have to get your pants off."

"No!" I clutched my pants with the available fingers of my right hand, and winced.

"Don't be silly. We have to finish your bath …others are waiting."

By this time, I was bolt upright. "Forget it! I'll do it myself. Just leave the sponge and the water and go away."

Those gentle smiles they'd tricked me with had masked devilish grins. "Sorry…it's against regulations. Now lift up."

"Not a chance!" I was beginning to panic.

"Do we have to get help? *We need some help over here…*"

Every nurse in the room looked over. They were all laughing. They'd obviously seen this show before.

"I'll help."

"Me too."

"Be right over."

But now that I was totally humiliated, the joke was over…for now.

"Here's the sponge," chuckled my nurse, as she left. "Don't spill the water, and try to keep the bandages as dry as you can."

I was there for two days, and I would have been perfectly comfortable if one or another of the nurses hadn't appeared at my side to wink at me every time they saw I was awake.

"Sponge bath, soldier?"

Suddenly a ship was leaving for North Africa, and I had to be on it. They hadn't gotten around to washing my clothes yet, so I had to wear them as they were. I didn't mind. I was going to a convalescent hospital where nobody would be likely to shoot at me, and with any luck at all, they'd let me bathe myself. Who could ask for more?

My disembarkation was the stuff motion pictures are made of. I appeared on deck with one hand bound up and the other arm in a sling, and still wearing that dramatically bloody shirt. After pausing a moment to squint into the Algerian sun, I strode manfully down the gangplank. There was a hush, and then I could hear a murmur swell through the crowd:

"Oh, the poor, poor boy."

"Look how bravely he bears his pain..."

"It's men like him who will save us from the Nazi menace!"

Okay, okay...so these comments were pretty much all in my head. But that doesn't mean that people weren't thinking them!

So I'm enjoying your last couple of letters from a comfortable convalescent camp far from the action. And I guess I'll be here a while.

Love,

Tommy

The Conquering Hero (in my head)

November 13, 1943

Kath,

It's a good thing for the war effort that getting shot is so risky, or everybody would want to do it. The convalescent hospital here is made up of a lot of tents, open to the desert breezes, where we get to sleep on real cots. Sure beats hell out of sacking out in freezing mud in the bottom of a trench! And our only duty is to recover our strength. None of the guys here are mortally wounded.

There's plenty of time here to think about the war.

In Sicily, it still seemed like a great adventure. Italy is serious business. Or maybe Sicily was just as dangerous, but we were too green to realize it. Anyway, it seemed like a lively introduction to the main act.

Every time I go into battle, I *intend* to do something amazing—something heroic. I'll rush in, single-handed, and save the day...and everybody will cheer. That's what I intend. Me and every other guy, I suppose.

But that's not why I fight when the battle is hot. It's because I'm not the only one out there. The other guys are counting on me. Those guys are my friends...I rely on them to back me up and I can't let them down. But that's not all. You know me too well. I have to admit that I can't let myself do less than any one of the others. It's in my nature.

And to tell the truth, none of us really believe we'll be the ones to get killed. It'll be somebody else. We're indestructible.

In your last letter, you asked about England. I guess my messages, while I was there, *were* pretty sketchy. I'll try to do better here:

When we landed there from Canada in spring of '40, we were greeted by a crowd of enthusiastic British dockworkers, holding up the first two fingers of their right hands, forming the "V" for victory.

A shipload of raw recruits stared.

"Look at them all!" somebody muttered. "What the hell are they doing?"

"I think it's some kind of sign."

"Sign? Sign of what?"

"I dunno...but it looks like something rude to me."

So right off the mark, you had a mass of welcoming dockworkers encouraging their allies ...and a deck packed with ignorant Canadians who thought they'd been insulted. We'd boarded the ship, intending to save Britain and win the war... and this was the welcome we got!

You can see how there was bound to be a bit of friction.

We were transported to a holding unit near Guildford for a while, expecting to reinforce the Canadians already in France. But the 48th High-landers had barely gotten 40 miles inland from St. Malo when the British front collapsed and they were ordered to evacuate *toot sweet*...back to the ship!

The division arrived safely back in England with all artillery intact. The British, on the other hand, who evacuated out of Dunkirk, didn't. The poor devils who got out at all, got back with nothing. Some arrived home in nothing but their underwear...and lucky to be alive to wear it!

The truth is, if the Germans had invaded England at that time, bloody little could have been done to stop them. The British army was nearly helpless. Artillery...equipment...all left behind in France. The 1st Canadian Division was the only formation left that was trained and equipped to defend Britain. Somehow, we had to make the Germans believe that the troops had gotten out of Dunkirk reasonably equipped and ready to fight them off, or they'd just saunter over and park their butts in Whitehall! And they had spies active along the English coast, eager to report any weakness.

So we staged what must have been one of the great farces of modern history.

First, they marched us through an English coastal town, for no particular reason that we could see. The lucky inhabitants enjoyed the spectacle of the regiment marching smartly through, in full battle gear. We were an impressive sight—unmistakably Canadian (the red badges, you know).

When we reached the other side of town, we found trucks ready and waiting.

"Onto the trucks, men," we were told. "Snap it up!"

"Hey...this is the life," I chuckled. "Limousine service."

The trucks sped off, depositing us at the outskirts of the next town, which we marched through in exactly the same way.

As we boarded the trucks that were waiting again outside that town, one of the guys called out to an officer:

"Hey, captain, what's all *this* in aid of?"

"Orders."

Orders. Okay...

That's pretty much how we spent the day. One town after another. The next morning, we prepared for more marching.

"No helmets today, boys," we were told. "Wear balmorals. And the Canada badges come off."

"What do you mean off?"

"The red badges. Cut them off. What don't you understand?"

"But then we'll look like just another pack of Brits!" We had our pride, after all.

"Never mind that—get them off. Make it snappy."

That day, we left several towns in the vicinity with the impression that a trained troop of Scottish Highlanders had marched on by.

That night, we were told we'd be marching again in the morning.

"And get those patches sewn back on your uniforms."

"You're kidding!" I blurted. He was gone. Apparently he wasn't kidding.

We pulled thread and needles out of our packs and started sewing.

DODGING SHELLS

For the next few weeks, we marched in and out of towns all along the south coast, changing our outfits like manic fashion queens. Anybody looking closely wouldn't have been fooled, but we kept up a brisk pace and at a glance any interested parties might drop a quick line to their Fuhrer reporting a lot of well-equipped Canadians on the move, protecting the coast, and an equal number of surprisingly well-equipped Brits. And all marching like they knew what they were doing.

Apparently it worked. The Jerries knew they'd given England a good trouncing but they must have thought there were a lot more trained troops where those came from, ready to go over and fight. So the invasion the British were worried about never happened—though the blitz was nasty business, I admit.

Sometimes we'd be sent to guard a factory along the coast, setting up Bren guns on the roof and watching for enemy planes. It wasn't very lively. We were ordered not to fire unless we were actually under attack...and that never happened. Occasionally we fired off a few illicit rounds anyway, which the Germans completely ignored—they were flying way too high to be in any danger from us. But it was a break from fashion parade duty and we got to eat at the factory canteens. It was still English food, but it least it wasn't English *army* food. There is a difference, though you have to look sharp, or you'll miss it. This was at about the time that Canadian troops stationed at Guildford rioted over being sentenced to mutton without the formality of a court martial.

They must have thought it'd be easier to hide our true numbers if we weren't stationed in a single army barracks, so they billeted us in a town called Littlehampton, not too far from Brighton. The army had confiscated several units at the end of a street of row housing, but it wasn't quite as comfy as it sounds; we were still five or six sweaty soldiers to a room, sacked out on straw paliasses on the floor. Even in England, summers can be warmish, and that was before we could compare it to summer in sunny Sicily and realize how lucky we were.

Eventually, the army realized that the way they were training us wasn't worth a damn. The German idea of Blitzkrieg—'lightning war'—was better. A *lot* better. So Monty had the Canadian Division trained Blitzkrieg-style. Our infantry could fight a motorized division to a stand-still by blocking them off wherever they turned...but we had to move fast! It took a lot of drilling. They had to keep us trying hard.

"Okay, men...we're doing another 'ten mile walk-and-run' today. Full equipment."

Groans all 'round. We were expected to walk and run the ten miles in under two hours...and our battle gear weighed about thirty pounds!

"And if we make the best time," added our sergeant, "I'll buy you a beer."

"Is that one beer to share, Sarge...or a beer for each?"

"Very funny. That you, Smitty? ...I thought so."

"Well that makes it interesting, eh guys?" There was a rush to gather equipment.

"Yeah...let's get crackin'. I can taste free beer already!"

We were supposed to take turns carrying the Bren guns, but some of the guys had trouble with the extra weight, and it was slowing us down. So when my turn was done, I refused to give up the heavy gun.

"Forget it," I said. "I'll go the distance." Nobody argued.

Alfie was carrying the other Bren gun. "I'll keep you company, Smitty," he offered.

It wasn't easy...those guns gained about ten pounds with every mile that went by. We'd stop every once in a while to catch our breath then run to catch up with the others. It was stretching the rules a bit, but it worked.

We were all making good time, but about ¾ mile from the end of the course, one of the guys—Bryce, it was—fell in the dirt.

"That's it," he gasped. "I'm done. I can't do it. Sorry, guys." Bryce was a nice enough fellow (he looked like Tyrone Power...you'd like him) but he wasn't awfully strong, physically.

We weren't about to give up our beers as easily as that. Somebody grabbed his gun and two others, one on each side of him, locked arms under Bryce's butt like a sling and *carried* him the rest of the way.

Alf and I only saw this when they panted in at the finish. Right after Bryce collapsed, Alf had turned to me, with a grin.

"Race you to the finish, Smitty!"

And we took off. When the platoon arrived, we were sprawled in the grass beside those Bren guns like we'd been left for dead. But no need for medics. A few magic words revived us:

"We did it! One hour and forty-two minutes! How about those beers?"

Oh...and I won the race with Alfie—but not by much. I did that ten miles in just over an hour and a half.

I can hear you disloyally wondering where all this strength and stamina is coming from. The 48th Highlanders is determined to have a premium regiment, so they won't accept anyone who measures under 5 foot 10 inches, and I'm barely that, stretched up tall! Well, in order to look smart on parade, we march with heights carefully graduated, having the tallest guys at the end of the line. (No, I'm not kidding...we're *that* vain.) That puts me right out in front. If I'm going to be conspicuous, it sure as hell isn't going to be as the runt of the litter! So I push myself harder than most of the other guys.

And I was about the youngest guy here, too. I signed up for all the courses the older guys couldn't be bothered with...physical training, unarmed combat, small arms...you've got to gain *something* from all that, right?

I didn't mind the gymnastics—I was good at that—but the Brits are really excited about cross-country running...and I wasn't. Stumping along for miles and hours in big boots and short pants...I felt like a fool! My lack of enthusiasm must have been pretty obvious. I lagged behind.

DODGING SHELLS

The training sergeant—a regular British army guy—dropped back with me. "C'mon Canada...can't you keep up?"

"I don't want to keep up." A bit sulky, I know. "This is stupid!"

"Well, don't worry about it, lad. We can't expect you to keep up with the English fellows because, you know, they're used to this sort of thing. They've developed the stamina for it. We know you Canadians don't have the same attitude toward physical training."

Naturally, I felt obliged to dispute this, but in order to do that I had to keep up with him. Soon we passed the other stragglers. *This running thing doesn't look like anything much,* I thought.

We passed the main body of men.

About a half mile from the end, the sergeant bellowed, "All right, men. Anyone who cares to show me what you've got...go!"

A handful of fellows put on a final burst of speed. Well, no bloody Englishman was going to get ahead of me, after what that damn' sergeant had said! I sprinted ahead, and kept on going to the finish line. It just about killed me.

Barely conscious, I waited for the sergeant to arrive. "Who has the stamina *now*?" I gasped.

He laughed, the bastard! "I knew I could make you do it." Hell isn't hot enough for guys like that.

Soon I could see a pattern...but I couldn't help myself. A trainer would say, in a suspiciously com-passionate tone, "All right, Canada...you ease off a bit. We know you're not used to all this..." And I would strain every muscle...take any risk...to prove they were wrong. It was a crummy, obvious trick.

And it worked. By the time they were done, I was designated to be a PT trainer myself.

One sport where I felt at a bit of a disadvantage was boxing. I'd had no experience at all in organized amateur boxing. But I did my best, and must have gotten fairly good at it, because near the end of the course, they pitted me against one of their best boxers!

I was flattered, I can tell you! I swaggered into the ring. *He can't hurt me!* I told myself, without believing it for a minute. Well, within the first few moments, he landed a punch square in my chest. It felt like I'd been hit by a wrecking ball. I thought I was going to die. But fate decided to give him another shot at me.

Like a fool, I charged right back at him. This time he hit me in the head. That actually didn't bother me much. In fact, all of a sudden, I found that I was beating him. I just couldn't believe it! I was fantastic! I bobbed...I weaved...he couldn't get as much as one punch in. *By god,* I thought—as much as I could think at all, that is—*it's taken me a while to hit my stride, but I'm amazing!* I was already picturing myself being declared World Boxing Champion when the referee stopped the fight:

"All right...all right...hold off, Canada. Can't you see? The poor chap broke his hand when he hit you in the head!"

I think he may have been faking...to avoid a good trouncing. But I've decided boxing may not be my calling after all. That punch in the chest really hurt.

DODGING SHELLS

What could be more dramatic than a bayonet? Kind of romantic, even, in a messy sort of way. I took the trouble to learn how to use one well, when I got the chance, and I guess I was pretty cocky about it.

We were trained by a stocky, competent sergeant major from an Irish Guards school. He seemed like such an old guy...he was maybe 35 or 40...and I was on the lookout for any opportunity to show him how a younger, fitter soldier (that would be me) could handle himself. Most of the time, he took it with a grain of salt; in fact, he didn't even seem to notice.

Toward the end of the course, he offered to show us how to defend against a bayonet attack with our bare hands. It seemed like an unlikely boast, but if there was anything in it, I was sure interested in learning the trick.

"Alright," he said. "I want somebody to come at me with a bayonet."

Nobody responded. "Don't be afraid," he grinned. "There's a mat over there...I'll throw you onto the mat. You'll be fine."

I sneered, and I guess he noticed. He chose me. "Canada...come at me with the bayonet."

"No, sir!" I refused. I wasn't going to attack an unarmed man with a bayonet!

"Why is that, Canada?"

"Well, if *I* come at you with a bayonet," I said, "I'll kill you." I was very sure.

"Soldier," he snapped. "I said you're to charge me with that bayonet...and don't hold back. That's an order!"

I turned to an officer. I had plenty to choose from. They were *all* officers—except me.

"You heard," I said, "He insists that I come at him. If I do..." I let them all consider the consequences. There were sober nods all round.

I was angry. He had put me in a terrible spot. I prepared myself to attack. I feinted, jumped back real quick, and then jammed the bayonet right into him.

Well...that was the way it was *supposed* to go. I managed the feinting part, and the jumping back part went well...and I even threw my weight into jamming the bayonet...

The next thing I knew, I was sailing through the air. I flew about fifteen feet and landed smack on the mat, just as he had promised—adding insult to lack of injury!

To make things worse, by the time I hit the ground, he was calmly explaining, "Now that was a good thrust! But let me explain this move so you can use it effectively..."

I'd tried to skewer him with a sharp weapon, and he acted like he was lecturing the ladies' auxiliary at a garden party. It was embarrassing.

After the class, he took me aside.

"Don't feel bad," he said. "That was an excellent thrust. Yes, very effective on that one. Very nice... very nice..."

I looked at him sourly. He obviously had some kind of supernatural powers. It wasn't fair.

"And don't kid yourself," he added. He held up his hand. I saw a nasty scar on the palm, and another on the back—clearly, a bayonet had passed through it.

DODGING SHELLS

"I trained the Irish Guards for years, and they could be mean bastards! They were in boot camp, and I guess it was rough on them, so they had to take it out on somebody. The odd guy got me, but after fifteen years of doing this...well, I don't get caught very often."

All the same, I'm not going to tell you how to disarm a man who's charging you with a bayonet. Don't ask me. If I couldn't do it...why should you be able to?

Just keep away from guys with bayonets.

Someday I'll show you a few other little tricks of unarmed combat that could be helpful for self-defence. For example, if you have a stick, there's a way of sticking it up under a guy's chin and into his throat that will make him stop and think. You don't usually carry a stick? Well, a newish pencil would work, in a pinch... *we* tend to be better supplied with sticks.

And don't try to strangle a guy with your bare hands. It's tougher than it sounds. You're better off pulling his helmet back and twisting, quick. If you do it right, the strap will snap his neck like a twig.

I can hear you complaining that few of your potential attackers are likely to be wearing helmets. Good point. Well, you could try using your thumbs to pop out his eyeball. That's a show-stopper in any kind of situation.

Wait till I get home—nobody's going to mess with my sister! At least...not more than once.

Of course, we couldn't train by throwing live grenades around. England is a small country. God knows what you could hit, without really meaning it. But sooner or later, we were going to have to do the job, and we needed to know what it feels like. So one day we gathered on one side of a carefully selected hill. Well, it was actually only a mound …maybe fifteen feet high, but it was high enough to protect us from the blasts, and there was nothing important on the other side. One by one, we were to pull the pin that arms the grenade and pitch it well over the crest of the hill where it was intended to explode, safely but with an impressively ground-moving blast.

"Where should we aim, Sergeant?"

"Don't get fancy. Just throw it over on the *other* side of the hill."

We laughed.

One by one, we had the experience of holding a live bomb in our hands…for a moment. I, for one, wasn't inclined to keep it with me any longer than was absolutely necessary.

Then it was Dave's turn. Dave was an able enough guy…but he was no ball player. Or he was scared. Or maybe his hand was sweaty. Whatever the reason, Dave pulled that pin and threw his grenade the required fifteen feet. But somehow, he threw the damned thing sideways. Yes, that grenade fell on *our* side of the hill.

"Shit!"

We had all watched the pitch, and we knew the end had come. I didn't notice what the other guys were doing, but in the absence of all other cover, I hit the ground and cowered behind my metal helmet. *Maybe if I can make myself small enough,* I thought, *it'll protect me.* I would have crawled right inside the thing, if I could've managed it...and don't think I didn't try!

When the dust settled, we found that no one had been hurt. It took a while before we could laugh about that one, but eventually we had to make Dave suffer over it, and that helped to distract us a bit.

Dave was always writing home to his wife, telling her every little thing. I'll lay odds he didn't tell her about *that*.

From time to time, when I was with my unit, 'schemes' were set up to simulate real battle conditions in order to train the troops and test the problems that might come up if an invading force made an assault. These were very elaborate, and as realistic as army command could make them. We called the most impressive of these the Horsham scheme.

The mandate was to defend Horsham, a town about 30 minutes from the coast, and the 48th Highlanders represented the attacking enemy force. We were to attack in the morning, and other units were set up ahead of us to defend the town. Because we were trained 'Blitzkrieg' style, I guess they thought we'd make the best Germans.

We took these schemes very seriously. Setting out from our base, thirty miles from the town, we marched all through the night, eating sandwiches for dinner on the road. By 5 a.m., we had marched right past the defenders, who were still dragging their asses out of bed, and Horsham was in mortal danger! That wasn't quite what the scheme planners had in mind.

We got the word:

"An (imaginary) brigade is in the town in front of you, blocking your advance. And there are opposing troops behind you. What are you going to do now?"

And the defending troops, who were now behind us, attacked.

"Hey! They're attacking! If we can't advance, we're screwed!" I have to tell you, we were seriously pissed off! We'd just marched thirty miles, fast and without a stop, and we were bushed! Now they were stacking the deck against us! How was *that* fair?

"Like hell we are! Fix bayonets!"

"But we could kill them."

"Then they'd better get the hell out of our way." Simulated battle be damned! We fixed bayonets and charged!

The defending troops took one look at those bayonets and suspected that we might have lost track of the point of this particular exercise. We were out for blood! They took out, on the double—with us hot on their heels.

One of the scheme judges eventually drove over to see what was going on, and he brought a brigadier general with him for good measure. When they came to a defile between two hills, they found the road blocked. We had rolled some large rocks down into the roadway.

"Halt!" We had left a guard.

"Here! Let us pass!" bellowed the judge.

"Sorry, sir...roadblock."

"You're not authorized to create a roadblock!"

"Too late, sir. Sorry, sir."

"I have a brigadier general here with me. Are you blind?"

"No sir." The guard saluted. "Welcome, sir."

"Well, then, are you going to move those bloody rocks?"

"No, sir!"

"Insubordinate morons," he muttered. He threw the jeep in reverse. And hit a rock.

While he'd been passing the time of day with the guard, we had rolled additional rocks right up behind the jeep, and we were on our way out of there.

We had ruined the scheme. It wasn't supposed to go that way. The word came:

"You are completely surrounded."

We were stunned. "We're not surrounded..."

"When they say we're surrounded, we're surrounded," said the officer in charge. "Those are the rules."

"So what now?"

"It's getting dark. We march."

So we marched back, through the opposing lines and headed for home. We marched all night. Again.

We'd marched thirty miles, fought all day, and were on our way back...36 hours without sleep. But we wouldn't stop. We must have been a sight... walking into each other...falling into ditches... stumbling...holding onto each other just to keep on our feet. But nobody dropped out. Nobody.

When we cleared the opposing lines and stopped for a break, we looked like corpses strewn along the side of the road. I saw one guy take his boots off to wipe the blood off his feet. He was one of the many who had complained that the scheme was a lot of trumped-up nonsense and a waste of time. But he wouldn't give up. He laced his boots back up and kept on marching.

When we were about ten miles from camp, the battalion trucks were sent to pick us up and drive us the rest of the way. When they found us, we were still marching.

But I haven't told you, yet, about one of our most dangerous assignments in England! We had been selected to test-drive U.S. battle helmets. They were a different shape from ours, and I guess the army wondered whether we could pick up some pointers for improvement.

That seems pretty safe, don't you think? Well, we thought so too. So we jammed on the new helmets and marched down the road. One helmet feels a lot like another when it's parked on your head, so we had pretty much forgotten about them when we heard the first shot. It came from a farm house near the road. We ignored it. Nobody would be shooting at us. Some farmer must be taking pot shots at a crow. Then another shot...this time from a hedge nearby.

Then a touring car came barrelling along the road, and we had to dive for the ditch. Hey! What the hell! It looked like he was aiming at *us*!

We finally realized that the loyal civilians in the neighbourhood were trying to kill us. They had mistaken the unfamiliar American headgear for German helmets...and they weren't going to let Jerry invade their countryside without putting up a fight!

DODGING SHELLS

I decided if anyone asked, my vote was going to be cast for staying with our own 'tin lids'...no matter what.

If we ignore this little misunderstanding, the English people were very good to us. Most of us were young and we were far from home. We had come over to help. And we had money to spend. It was an endearing combination.

And the place where we felt most welcome was, of course, the local pub. Any local pub. There's nothing like them at home. I've been in Toronto beer parlours the odd time (only to fetch somebody out, you understand), and they tend to be dingy, cheerless places with disapproval built in, somehow. The pubs in England are homes away from home; the word 'jolly' was invented to describe the atmosphere. And no one questioned our right to down a pint, or several.

Of course if you put soldiers, sailors and airmen of different nations in one room, however jolly, you're going to see fights. Fellows in their cups can be sensitive about the smallest things. Take, for example, one of our favourite songs:

"There'll always be an England,
And England will be free...
As long as there are Canadian troops
Crossing o'er the sea."

Apparently the Brits favour a different version, and they can get real touchy about it.

My record, in England was…well…a bit spotty. In fact, my rank went up and down like a yo-yo, jumping around between private and corporal, with pit stops at lance corporal. Nothing big—just silly kid pranks and going AWOL from time to time. The army frowns on that brand of levity. I wasn't planning to make a career of the army anyway, so I didn't take these demotions very seriously.

I did have one real scare. After I first made corporal, I was in charge of an ack-ack group. I was supposed to get them out by dawn one day, and I slept late. I felt bad about it, but it was only a manoeuvre…how serious could it be? Well, I'll tell you. When they read the charge, I broke into a cold sweat: "failure to do your duty in the face of the enemy"! That is really, *really* bad. Apparently, there doesn't have to actually be an enemy in the vicinity for the charge to stick. I could have been court-martialled!

I was lucky. They only busted me back to private. But it scared the hell out of me. I was seventeen years old at the time.

Finally, last December, we got our orders to move up to Scotland…where we would continue to train and wait to be deployed.

We spent the day before Christmas training for an assault landing. Our assault vessel pulled up to the beach at night but couldn't get in close to the shore, so we had to jump out into freezing water up to our bellies. We charged across the beach, executing assault manoeuvres, and scaled a cliff, arriving at the top cold and exhausted.

DODGING SHELLS

"All right men," barked the officer. "We're going to stop here."

We all flopped down...and found ourselves in the middle of a bog! Before long, two or three inches of water seeped into the hollows where our bodies lay, soaking whatever fragments of our duds we had managed to keep dry.

Some Christmas Eve, I thought. *Bah! Humbug.*

How was I to know that some intuitive soul was preparing us for conditions in 'sunny' Italy?

The next day, after we had dried off and thawed out, they served us a real Christmas dinner! There was beer, served in a big tin wash bucket...and turkey...and venison. It was a feast worthy of Dickens.

Wait—venison? Somebody, in the throes of the Christmas Spirit, had gone out and shot a couple of the King's Deer. (I guess they're *all* the King's Deer. At least, no one suggested that this one had been branded, or wearing a little sign or anything.) And it seems that the King gets a bit touchy about that kind of thing. When the wrong people found out, all hell broke loose. There were reprimands and outrage and great drama, but the punishment was confined to fines. They probably let us off easy because they figured we were just ignorant Canadians, and accustomed to shooting wild game out of our kitchen windows.

Anyway, it was worth it.

Speaking of Christmas...if you want to send me a gift, send a watch.

Suppose, for a second, that the platoon is spread out over a hillside. Our orders are to attack at fourteen hundred hours. Each man keeps an eye on his watch. Then:

"Hey, Mack! What time is it?" This is a guy who doesn't have a watch. Could be me.

Mack hears. The Germans hear. The Germans shoot at the loud guys who don't have watches.

Send a watch.

Your convalescent brother,

Tommy

December 18, 1943

Kath,

Thanks for the watch! It's a beauty.

We don't stand much on ceremony here... packages are always opened as soon as they're received. Even Christmas presents. But I'll wind it in your honour on the 25th. How's that?

I've had a couple of months now to get accustomed to this hole in my shoulder and it doesn't hold my attention the way it did originally. In fact, I find myself forgetting it for minutes at a time.

At first, they had to examine the wound and change the dressing constantly to prevent infection and keep out the damned desert sand that sneaks into the most inconvenient places. I felt like a broken tool that's been patched back together. Everybody was waiting for the glue to dry so they could see if the repair was going to hold.

Eventually, I eased back into exercising the arm every day and they just checked the wound from time to time to make sure it wasn't going maggoty or anything. To tell the truth, I was getting eager to get back to my unit. The guys were fighting through some bad patches and they needed me.

Besides, the desert is boring.

A couple of days ago, I was being checked by the doctor. He poked. He prodded. "So, how are you finding the arm?" he asked.

"No problem, doc. It's right there…attached to my shoulder. I can't miss it."

He barely cracked a smile. Tough audience.

"It's looking good…but how's it working?"

"Not bad at all! Look," I said. "I can already raise it to here…" I gingerly raised my damaged arm up in front of me, to shoulder level, and winced. "But who knows when I'll be able to do *this*!" I added, lifting it high in the air and waggling it around, with a grin.

So I'm writing this from a holding unit in Italy while I wait to re-join my regiment. But I still think that doctor was laughing inside.

I haven't let even this short stopover go to waste, though. I made time to represent our country at one of the local watering holes last night. It's important that we hold up our end, because there are a lot of Yankees here, and they get kind of frisky if they're not kept in order.

When he realized that I was a Canadian, I was favoured by one of our American neighbours with a little poem. His delivery was a bit sloppy because he'd been drinking, but it went something like this:

"Here's to the American eagle,
That high and lofty bird…
Flies over the broad plains of Canada
And drops an American turd."

DODGING SHELLS

He was so proud of himself that I had to return the honour. I stood, relatively steadily, and raised my glass:

"And here's to the broad plains of Canada
On the other side of the ditch.
We want none of the turds from your bald-headed birds,
You American son of a bitch!"

Now, who could have guessed that my poetic friend was the sensitive type? He took offence at my description of his mother...or maybe of the eagle ...and he and a few of his friends started swinging. Fortunately, they'd spent the earlier part of the evening insulting all the British soldiers in the room, so I had plenty of back-up. My arm got an impromptu workout, and a good time was had by all.

This gift for poetry is something I inherited from Dad. Did he ever tell you why he came to Canada? He may have thought the story was inappropriate for a young girl's ears without editing out the good bits. Fortunately, your brother is without conscience, so here it is:

We never knew much of anything about Dad's people in England. Well, they're pretty flush, really; country squires, as a matter of fact. They own a bunch of pubs. Anyway, when he was twenty-two years old, they decided he should marry a local minister's daughter. I guess they thought it would slap a veneer of respectability on the family. She was a nice enough girl, I guess, but he wasn't ready

111

to settle down, and didn't appreciate the pressure his folks were putting on him to polish up the family image.

You know Dad—even then, he could never say no directly. He spent some time with the girl, hoping she'd realize that they were wrong for each other. But he was just too damn charming. She began to get altogether too fond of him, and finally insisted that he declare his intentions. Being something of a common man's poet, he leaned in close and murmured:

"I don't know much about lovin', lass,
But I'll feel your bum for a start."

To give her credit, the girl immediately grasped the message he was trying to send. He was definitely not husband material. Unfortunately, she was offended enough to complain to her old dad, who was no poet at all. Word got around, and it was clear that the subtlety of Dad's exit strategy was appreciated by no one. By the time the family suggested that Dad get out of England, he was quite ready to go, realizing that his particular sense of humour needed the soil of a newer, younger country to truly bloom. They even offered him a small stipend to *stay* out. (Remember Uncle Harry, who used to drop by briefly from time to time, pearl grey spats and all? He was the one who delivered the periodic bribe money; god knows what paranoia stopped them from simply dropping it in the mail.)

I did stop off to visit his family for a few days when I first got to England. I guess I forgot to mention it because I'm not sure I come off looking very good in the story.

I dropped in on Dad's older brother Harry and his family. He's a Reeve or Mayor or something, and believe it or not, he still wears spats, too, when he struts around town. Everyone was pleasant and oh, so polite, but the tour dragged a bit until he took me to see the local pub—one of theirs, it was. I met Dad's stepmother—she runs the place, and I got the idea that she's the one who has all the business know-how. I think she used to be a barmaid, so she's accustomed to it. They're lucky to have her. I don't see how the family could stay afloat long on spats and etiquette alone.

I was beginning to enjoy the idea of a family pub, but when I offered to pay for a round of drinks—it seemed only fair—I noticed that silence fell and everybody looked distressed...like they'd swallowed something live and wiggly and were way too classy to mention it. I insisted, and the money changed hands gingerly. You'd think it had turned into dried dog turds when I wasn't looking.

As the pub filled up, Uncle Harry began introducing me to their friends and acquaintances.

"This is my brother Fred's son. Fred's the one who went out west to Canada, y'know."

By the time he ran this through the third time, it started sounding like:

This is my good-for-nothing brother Fred's son. He's the one we shipped out to the colonies so he couldn't continue to embarrass us.

I know...I know...there's an element of truth in it. But he didn't have to *say* it! Okay, he didn't actually say it. But I suspected that it's what he meant. And I resented it.

Dad's sister Elsie had come into the pub to meet me. She'd married a working man (god forbid!) and they lived a small distance outside town. I got the distinct impression that the family disapproved of her marriage and avoided her when they could. That was enough to make Elsie my favourite, so I spent the remainder of my leave with her, ignoring all pleas to join the rest of the family.

I never saw them again. Now that I think about it, I guess I might have had a bit of a chip on my shoulder. They were nice enough people and they probably didn't mean any harm. But their particular note of genteel superiority doesn't play well to a Canadian ear...and I was too young and too raw to overlook it.

As for my brash show of independence—insisting on paying for beers in my own family's pub—well, short of telling me not to be such a lout, I really don't know what they could have done. In my own defence: I was sixteen years old. What the hell did I know?

But I don't think I'll go back.

Merry Christmas, Sis. It was always my very favourite holiday, and you're going to have to enjoy it for both of us again this year.

Have a wonderful time! Wish I was there...

Wait! Maybe at the stroke of midnight on Christmas Eve, I'll be able to show up briefly as a shadowy Spirit of Christmas Absent.

Nah...forget it. That's just kind of creepy.

Your considerate brother,
Tommy

January 10, 1944

Kath,

I hope you had a great Christmas. Really. I do. Mine stunk.

No kidding. It stunk. And the smell was the best part.

I spent Christmas in a place we've come to call Cemetery Hill. Sounds like field headquarters for Scrooge's Ghost of Christmas Future, doesn't it? Well, it's not.

A couple of days before Christmas, we were ordered to take and hold a ridge overlooking the roads supplying the Germans who were defending a town called Ortona, god only knows why. From there, our guys would be able to rain artillery fire down on supply trucks whenever the mood moved us, and cut off the Jerries' supply of sauerkraut. *That* should drive them out of town!

Taking the ridge turned out to be easier than it looked. We snuck up a muddy footpath in the dead of night. We would be inside enemy lines, and we all knew if we bumped into a German patrol on that narrow trail, we wouldn't stand a chance. A fire-fight from a single-file formation would be a disaster—the battalion could be wiped out. There hadn't even been time for reconnaissance. We could only hope the Germans would be staying in out of the rain.

DODGING SHELLS

That rain was pissing down, the track was slippery and invisible, and the price of straying off it was a wallow in ankle-deep mud. It was pitch black, lit only from time to time, for our travelling convenience, by distant artillery fire...ours and Jerry's. It took us over three hours, at a shuffle—starting, stopping, feeling our way—to struggle to the top of the ridge. We were soaked to the skin, but the cold rain slapping down on the leaves around us helped to mask the tell-tale sounds four hundred men tried not to make.

After an hour or so, a German prisoner straggled past us toward the back of the line, then another, so there must have been *some* kind of action going on further up the trail. They must have been threatened with a particularly unappealing death, because they didn't make a sound as they passed. But we didn't feel one bit more comfortable, as we slogged along, knowing they had been there.

We arrived in time for the day before Christmas. Not a shot had been fired.

"So..." somebody whispered, "Where are our hosts?"

"They must have turned in for the night."

"You'd think they'd be here to greet us...we plan to stay a while."

"I guess they don't know we're here."

We didn't mind. Like good guests, we dug our trenches and settled in without disturbing them unnecessarily.

Holding the ridge was trickier. Once we got there, we were stranded, a mile inside the German lines, so we were surrounded by enemy troops. And we only had the small arms, ammo and rations we had carried up that miserable trail: Tommy guns, Bren guns, grenades. Just the kind of things you'd pack in a suitcase for any holiday jaunt—nothing too bulky.

It was fairly quiet the first day.

"We have to be surrounded by Jerries," muttered the guy next to me. "Where the hell are they?"

"You *looking* for their attention, or what?" I asked. Wet socks make me testy.

"Well, no...I only wondered."

I relented a little. "Maybe they're trimming their tree or something. I think the Germans invented the Christmas tree..."

"Who cares?" This came from another guy nearby. I guess he wasn't in the mood to hear anything good about the Germans.

"Well, I'm just saying."

"They sure aren't singing carols, or we'd hear them!"

A few German snipers were practicing their shots, and there was machine gun fire from nearby houses, but we ignored it. We had to preserve our ammunition. There was no way to get supplies to us, and the tanks were bogged down in the mud somewhere. We were on our own.

We could only stay put and wait. That sounds a lot cozier than it felt. It was bloody cold, lying in those waterlogged trenches, and the rain kept right on falling, eventually petering out to an icy drizzle. We had finally been issued our winter uniforms—with long pants, and puttees buckled on to keep the mud from oozing up our legs. So at least we didn't have to lie there in our short pants and shirt sleeves this time. We actually had bomber jackets and sweaters...and don't think we weren't grateful. But when they were wet through, we were still left shivering in our custom built mud puddles. And we'd had no chance to arrange anything in the way of toilet facilities. That hospital in Egypt was looking better and better in my memory, and I wondered why I'd been so damned eager to leave it.

"Hey!" I bitched, to nobody in particular, "Didn't the bigwigs promise us we'd be home by Christmas this year...again? What happened with that?"

"Piss off!"

I guess everybody was a bit edgy.

The next morning, all hell broke loose. The Germans laid on the mortar and artillery fire, to say nothing of tossing around some mean cannon shells. They were bent on destroying the whole lot of us. This seemed downright unneighbourly, so we spent the day trying to kill them back. Some Christmas! Reinforcements couldn't reach us and we couldn't—and wouldn't—withdraw, so it was getting pretty lonely out there despite all the attention we were getting from the Jerries.

When night fell, they would occasionally try to sneak through our lines, a few at a time. They might only have meant to pay a friendly yuletide visit, and if they hadn't been heavily armed with machine and submachine guns, we might have been more welcoming. But we couldn't trust them not to attack us from the rear—it had been known to happen—so I'm afraid they got a grumpy reception.

At about nine o'clock (I know…because I have a watch!) headquarters was finally able to use the same trail we had slithered up to get rations and ammunition to us, and some light mortars. If they hadn't, we might have been wiped out. Our day's sport had nearly drained our supply of ammo, and I don't think mud balls would have held the enemy off for long. Sis, I don't want you to think I don't appreciate the watch. I do. I really do. But I could sure have used a tank as well—something in the way of a reconditioned Sherman would have been nice. I only mention this…for the next time.

Hey! Christmas wasn't all bad.

Around dinner time, things eased off a bit, and I pulled a little bag out of my pack.

"Look, guys. My sister sent me these…they're my favourites."

"So…what are they?"

"They're *Christmas* candies. You know. Those hard stripey ones that look like little pillows."

"And you brought them up here?"

"Yeah…I slipped a few into my pack when we were heading out."

"You're kidding."

"No…they're Christmas candies."

"But nobody actually eats those things!"

"I do."

"Aren't they soggy by now?"

"A little…look, do you want one, or not?"

"No. Thanks." Their loss. They had just passed up the only Christmas feast we were going to get.

Thanks, Sis…you're a honey!

DODGING SHELLS

The next day was really cold, but at least it was dry. German shells were still pounding down right among us. *Crump! Crump!* It was irritating.

"Look over there—right beyond our perimeter."

"Yeah. Germans. What a surprise."

"But it seems like there are more. Doesn't it look like there are more?"

"Maybe..."

"There are a lot more."

"You're right. Looks like they're massing over there...getting ready to drop in, uninvited. Better tell the captain." It turned out it was the paratroopers again. Wherever the Canadians are sent, they seem to show up, and if we don't watch it, people are going to start talking about us...

"Yeah. Well, their timing stinks!" We had no ammunition to spare for a rousing welcome...we were running short again and begrudged every bullet and grenade we had to send their way.

I was starting to consider fashioning a slingshot and gathering some stones when I heard the word "Tanks!" There must have been a Boxing Day sale at the used tank store, because not one but three very serviceable Sherman tanks appeared at the top of the same dirt trail that had brought us to that god-forsaken place. While we were freezing our asses off overnight, the ground had been freezing too, and they were finally able to make the climb. Some god must have been listening to our prayers because, contrary to all common sense, the Germans never did block that pass.

"We're okay, boys," I shouted. "The tanks are here!"

I'm sure I heard a voice somewhere behind me mutter something that sounded like "It's about time," but I didn't look around. The timing suited me just fine. I was still alive and no major parts were missing.

Those tanks didn't stop to chat; they roared through our front lines, guns blasting, and our paratrooper pals bolted like jackrabbits fleeing the hasenpfeffer pot!

"C'mon, guys...we've rested enough. Fall in!"

They didn't have to tell us twice. The Jerries had been dumping lethal crap on us for days, and we were going to get even! We took off after the tanks, and any German unlucky enough to be in our path couldn't expect to get a break.

When we were done, the battlefield was littered with bodies. There were only a few casualties among the Highlanders, but there were a whole lot of dead Germans, so we had to put off celebrating in order to bury them before they started to stink (and believe me, even the reek of so much blood was no treat.) We dug a huge grave, and dumped the lot in. It was brutal, but it was as much as they could have expected. We were glad we were alive and we were glad they were dead. Then we all found some-thing else to do while our chaplain murmured a few words over the grave. It was Padre East who named the place Cemetery Hill.

Our Padre East is one of those quiet Christians who give religion a good name. If anybody could keep evil away, it would be him. He tries to be everywhere, all the time, helping in whatever way he can. On foot or on a motorcycle, he's up and down the line, giving an encouraging word here and carrying a rifle for a tired soldier there. I've even seen him pick up a shovel and dig a grave himself rather than ask for help from exhausted soldiers, though it was clear he was so tired he could hardly stand up to hold the burial service.

He and I hadn't gotten off to a great start. His first sermon in Sicily was supposed to be encouraging:

"Remember, boys," he assured us, "We're fighting for the right!"

I couldn't resist putting my two cents in. "So... you mean we're right, then, and the Germans are wrong?" I asked.

"Of course."

"You've got to be kidding! We're all out here trying to *kill* people. How can that be right?"

He looked kind of sad and I was almost sorry I'd brought it up.

"Of course that's true," he admitted. "There's nothing right about it." Then he grinned at me. "But maybe you'll feel better remembering that God knows we're a little less wrong than they are."

Our position on the ridge was solid now and when the Jerries realized they'd soon be surrounded, they tip-toed out of Ortona in the dead of night and beat it north up the coast road while it was still open. Of course, we can't take *all* the credit. We hear there'd been brutal fighting in the streets between the Germans and our western Canada troops for days. I'll admit that might have had something to do with their decision to clear out too.

You'd think that's about as much fun as a body could take for one Christmas season. But within a couple of days we were sent to clean the Jerries out of a couple of small towns nearby. On the way to our second target of the day, the skies opened up and a blanket of shells slammed right down on the road. Men were falling everywhere…being tossed through the air like tattered bean bags. Anyone who didn't dive for the scratty little ditch was hit, and any new reinforcements didn't have a chance …their reactions were just not quick enough yet.

Geez, I thought…*Those Germans can really hold a grudge!*

Then, all of a sudden, it stopped. And the rumours started creeping around.

"Hey, Smitty."

"Yeah?"

"I hear it was friendly fire."

"Like hell! Look at this mess…"

"No kidding. They say a couple of British field regiments were laying down an artillery barrage to help us out…and they fired short. Somebody called back and stopped it."

"British."

"Yeah."

"For Chrissake, we haven't seen hide nor hair of the Brits this whole time and now they show up? I thought we'd left them all behind months ago."

"Well…a few of them must have run to catch up."

"And *this* is how they help? They could have saved themselves the bother!"

All the same, we held both villages by nightfall.

So, then…how was *your* Christmas?

Expecting full details,
Tommy

February 19, 1944

Kath,

I finally got your great Christmas letters! I wonder if you realize how important it is to know that there's still something normal back there to fight for.

And I got the gift you sent along. But when I opened the package, I wasn't alone. I had an audience.

"Hey, Smitty...what the hell is that blue thing?"

"Um..." I said, "I think my sister knit it."

"Nice. What is it?"

"You're so interested..." I snapped. "*You* figure it out." I was a tiny bit embarrassed. I didn't know *what* it was.

"Well...it kinda looks like a mitten."

"Just one?"

"There's no thumb."

We all examined it, gingerly. It was stretchy. Hmmm.

"There's a hole in it. On purpose, I think."

Silence. Then snickering.

"Okay, okay," I insisted. "What's so funny?"

"Well, I don't know why it has to stretch so damn' big...but I think it's a pecker-warmer!"

"Hey!" I reminded them. "My *sister!*"

By the time somebody recognized that it was something they call a balaclava—to wear over your head—I'd had to threaten two of the most insistent comics with serious physical pain in order to curb their imaginations.

Never mind. It keeps my ears and neck real cozy when it snows. And it's blue, like my puttees...that's nice. But next time, warn me, will you?

You mentioned cigarettes. No, I didn't get any cigarettes. I've *never* gotten any cigarettes. None. But I'm sure the guys behind the lines appreciated them. *Way* behind the lines. Who knows...maybe they thought we were goners anyway, so why waste perfectly good fags. I figure I'm lucky I got the watch...maybe because it was wrapped in toilet paper. Behind the lines, they've got plenty of toilet paper, so they don't need ours. (Thanks for the toilet paper, by the way.) And the candies...well, I guess nobody wanted them back there either.

Mostly, I make do with *Victory cigarettes, troops-for-the-use-of.* They're made especially for us in India from camel dung...or the dung of sacred cattle, maybe. We're not sure which, but a betting man can always get some action going on that point. Our matches don't stay lit worth a goddam, but occasionally we get the chance to liberate a stash of Italian sulphur matches. They won't go out, but when they're used in the field, under cover, they'll choke you half to death. Makes it hard to choose how you want your position revealed to the Germans—by the flame at night, by the smoke during the day, or by the coughing pretty much any time at all.

We keep pushing at the Jerries, and they keep pushing back. They're making us fight for every inch of ground, and I don't know why. It's all mud, and I would have thought they'd be glad to get rid of it. But no! They've ripped up the rail lines and blown up the roads and bridges and gone 'way out of their way to make us feel unwelcome. It's common at any time to come across unexploded shells and mortar bombs sticking out of the mud. Some are duds and others have only landed at an awkward angle that spared the detonating fuse from igniting. But the German engineers, rascals that they are, sometimes booby trap these babies as a little surprise for us. We've learned to avoid them.

Did I mention mud? Marching here is like mucking across the pitted top of a particularly nasty chocolate cake decorated with bombed out buildings, rubble and shattered olive trees. And when the tangled wire of the vineyards trips us up, what we fall into is sure not icing.

Sometimes it snows here, but most often it rains. It rains a lot. The rain soaks right through your greatcoat (yeah, I had a greatcoat—for a while) then freezes stiff. It's awkward as hell, and downright dangerous in a battle, so it was no great loss when it disappeared. I know, I know...I'd lose my head if it wasn't tacked on. I hear you.

Never mind...right now, I have a blanket! And I can sometimes keep it fairly dry, too, wrapped in my ground sheet—that's rubberized. A dryish blanket. There's luxury for you!

There haven't been any major battles since Christmas—only hundreds of deadly little skir-mishes with those pig-headed Germans. But I've noticed something interesting. The guys who are killed in minor battles are just as dead as they would be if they were making headlines.

DODGING SHELLS

I found myself in a jam during that sort of battle not too long ago. I'd gotten way too close to the enemy lines when they laid on some really impressive fire power. It was late, but not dark enough to get out of there unnoticed, so I crawled into a friendly neighbourhood foxhole and prepared to spend the night. I jammed my helmet under my hip to keep me out of the rain water puddling in the bottom of the hole (it was raining...of course it was) and jammed myself against the side, hunching down below ground level to avoid the majority of whatever was hissing and howling through the air above me. That was as good as it was going to get for a while, so I fell asleep. (It's a gift.) I woke up early next morning, when one of our guys, surging forward, overlooked the trench and stepped on my head as he ran by. It hurt like hell, but my first thought was: *Hey! That hurts... I must still be alive.*

You see...we're easily pleased, over here.

And the guy who stepped on me barely broke his stride. I've seen guys charging the enemy under fire blown right off their feet by a grenade, bounce right back up again and hit the ground running. Hell, I've seen a guy get his head blown clean off by a shell and keep right on running. But not far.

Death has gotten familiar...we know it's part of the 'cost of doing business'. Lacking better cover, I've stretched out behind a dead body and braced my gun on the corpse for a good shot. It's hard to be picky under those conditions, but a big, solid German corpse would always be my choice.

Still, sometimes we stumble over something that flashes a light on the kind of world we're living in. Grant was a new guy in our platoon—a quiet guy, always reading when he could get a book in his hands. He didn't exactly fit in with the gang but he was a good sport and he never lost his temper. Maybe it was because of this—maybe he didn't seem quite as tough as the others—we were always making him the butt of some stupid prank or other, when things were slack and boredom set in.

The first time Grant was out on a night patrol with us, we had snuck right up near where the Germans had been. It appeared that they'd pulled back, but we dug ourselves pits and settled in for a bit to make sure. Grant had more guts than we'd given him credit for—or maybe he was trying to prove himself to us—because he was by himself, out in front.

I was sharing cover with Charlie, and not altogether happy about it, because Charlie was a hotshot and a smart ass. Like me...but irritating.

"Look at him, out there," hissed Charlie, after we'd been huddled there for a while. "I bet he's pissing his pants." We were fairly sure by then that the Germans had moved on.

"He's fine," I whispered. "What do you care?"

"Watch. I'm going to scare hell out of him."

"What are you going to do, for Chrissake? Leave him alone. We're about done here. We need to move forward."

"Shut up and watch." Charlie slithered out and crept over behind Grant, who was watching out front. Suddenly, I saw Charlie's shadow rise up against the night sky. He shoved his gun in Grant's back and snarled, *"Hände hoch!"*

DODGING SHELLS

Grant wheeled around, his Tommy gun spraying bullets in an arc.

A Tommy gun packs quite a wallop. When a guy is hit by a .45 slug, he usually goes down...and stays down. Charlie took four in the stomach. He wasn't getting up.

I guess Charlie expected Grant to throw his hands up and surrender. Then we would all have had a good laugh at his expense. He misjudged his man. It was a hell of a price to pay for a practical joke gone bad.

In time, you get used to getting shot at... shelled...bombed. But you never forget to take cover. Still, there are things you just don't want to do in a trench...

We were dug in at the bottom of a hill and we knew the Germans had established themselves with some large hardware on the other side of the hill crest, so we weren't going anywhere. Time passed...and nature called. Urgently.

"Damn!" I muttered. "I have to take a dump."

"Not here, you don't." A unanimous reply.

"Well, what do you expect me to do?"

"I don't care, but you're not doing it here."

"It's too risky...I could get shot!"

"Tough."

I couldn't wait to negotiate. I slipped out of the trench and crept about forty feet away. Digging a discreet hole, I squatted...and immediately, the ear-splitting screech of Moaning Minnies shattered my peace of mind and changed my plans. I beat it back to the trench as fast as my feet would carry me.

As soon as the shells stopped falling—and it was hardly soon enough—I tried again. Once more, I had barely crouched over my latrine hole when the shells began shrieking down.

"Shit!" I blurted, and I wasn't even *trying* to be ironic.

I tore back to the trench and dove in. Fear of the shelling clenched my innards while I ran, but as soon as I was in no danger of being blown away... well, when the shelling stopped, I was back out and headed for the latrine hole again.

By the time this farce had played out a couple more times, I was sure that the entire German army was sitting up on that ridge, *watching* for me! They were aiming those mortars directly at me, and the sadistic bastards were probably laughing them-selves sick over it.

My trench mates finally realized that I couldn't go out there again; it would be suicide. They couldn't say I hadn't tried. Somebody handed me a small sack—handy for use as a pillow, but now judged disposable—and they looked away.

Any day we can capture some transportation is a good day. And the day we captured a German half-track was a very good day. It was as big as some of our tanks, and carried huge guns that blasted as it barged along the road towards us. But we lobbed grenades at it, disabling Germans until there was nobody left to drive, and it stopped. The dead and dying Jerries were carted away, and the big truck was ours.

We always try to keep a few grenades around, hanging from our uniform webbing, because they're so damn' handy. There are pineapple grenades that explode into about eighty pieces of deadly metal shrapnel—excellent, as long as you don't hold them too long before pitching them at a target, because once the pin is pulled...well, you can't push it back in again. Bakelite grenades are different—they release phosphorus, which smokes like hell and can help to screen an attack. As a bonus, the concussion will stun anybody in the area and kill the ones with the bad luck to be too close to impact. And thrown into an enclosed space, they're especially nasty because a phosphorus fire just won't go out. Anybody in there with one will get burned to an ugly black crisp. Fortunately, they're a bit safer for the pitcher because they are detonated by a lead weight fastened to a ribbon. When you throw one of these babies, the lead weight drags on the ribbon, pulling it out and exploding the bomb. It can't explode in your hand...which is a big bonus.

Against the half-track, we used pineapple grenades.

It was getting dark and beginning to rain, and the loss of one half-track hadn't discouraged the Germans nearly enough, because shells kept on landing all around us. But, always on the watch for an advantage, I noticed that they were not falling *under* the truck. All things considered, it looked like the safest place to be...and the driest. So I crawled under the brute and slept until morning.

I was jolted awake by the roar of an engine. Bolting up, I smashed my head on the undercarriage of my hideaway...but that was the least of my problems. Somebody had started the engine and was driving the truck away! Rapidly considering my alternatives, I rejected the one that involved rolling out on the off chance that the tracks might not crush me like a bug. Instead, I chose to lie real still and pray that this would not be the last stupid thing I'd ever do. It had seemed like such a good idea at the time...

I must have made the right decision because the driver steered straight ahead and the truck rolled away, leaving me lying there, intact. I immediately knocked one more option off my list of safe places to shelter from enemy attack.

After almost every battle, there are wounded left behind who have to be evacuated. I guess, in a perfect world, the able bodied would be lining up for the chance to rescue the disabled. The truth is, nobody's eager to volunteer. If you come out alive, you just want to keep your head down and enjoy one more lucky break. It seems downright foolhardy to wander back over the battle ground, under fire, carrying the guys fate had frowned on. But it has to be done. I'd want somebody to do it for me.

Often the one out there looking for the wounded and the dead is Padre East, who seems to lead a charmed life. The Padre is unarmed, so he needs to take a guard on these forays. For some reason, he has an annoying habit of asking *me*. And you can be sure when I'm wandering around with him and the bombs are still falling, I take cover where I can find it. But the padre is fearless. Well, I guess it's alright for him...he can call in special favours from heaven on the strength of his good acts. But I'm not sure that most of my own acts are good enough to rate protection from anything more lethal than a light breeze. I figure I'm pretty much on my own out there, and I often wish he'd choose somebody else for a change.

While we're on the topic of jobs nobody wants to do...burying dead guys is right up there, near the top of the list. When we first arrived here, I thought, *I'm a soldier—I don't **do** that kind of stuff.*

Wrong. I don't know who I thought *would* do it, but I soon found out. It's one of our jobs, and when your turn comes up, there's no dodging it.

The first time I was sent out on burial detail, we were ordered to bury a bunch of dead Germans. It was Sicily, it was summertime, and they were stinking up the place. First we dug the graves, and you can believe we didn't dig them any bigger than we had to. It was hot, we were tired, and the dead guys were the ones getting in out of the damned sun! Then we dumped the bodies in and covered them decently with dirt, ready for Padre East to say a few words. Except for one guy.

"Goddammit!" I said, to no one in particular. "The bloody fool died with his right arm sprawled out, and he's stiffened up like that. He won't fit!"

"You'll have to keep digging," suggested the misguided gravedigger to my left.

"Like hell I will!" There was no way I was going to dig a bigger hole—the sweat was already dripping off my face—and the German wasn't even *trying* to co-operate. I looked around. "Where's the padre?"

"He's not here yet. He's on his way..."

"Quick...come here and give me a hand!" I bashed the arm a few times with the shovel to break the bone, and we stomped it in a bit so we could push the body down into the hole.

"What the hell," I muttered. "He won't care. He's dead."

But I think Padre East might have cared. I threw a few shovelfuls of dirt into the grave to cover the body and spare him the knowledge.

With us so intent on nudging the Germans northward and them digging in their heels, every shabby little inch of real estate is disputed. One night, I was crouched in a slit trench, guarding one approach to a sorry, shell-pocked excuse for a shack on the other side of a shallow gully. The place had been hotly contested. First held by the Germans …then taken by our boys…driven out by the Germans again…and so it went. This night, a Canadian squad was in possession, and all the Jerries in the neighbourhood were firing away at it like the bad sports they are. During a momentary lull in the action, I heard a Canadian voice ring out:

"If you wanted this bloody house so bad…why the hell didn't you keep it?"

There was silence for a moment, and then a guttural voice responded with a distinct German accent.

"Fock you!"

Toward the end of January, the adjutant sent for me.

"Corporal, there's a bad patch up ahead," he said, "but we haven't been taking any prisoners for a while. We need to get up there and bring back some prisoners so we can find out what we're dealing with."

"Yeah," I agreed. "That would be good." *Maybe,* I hoped, *he only wanted somebody to chat with.*

"I want you to take a scouting patrol in and see how we can get the job done."

Oh, great. "Why me? My company hasn't been out there. I haven't even seen the area. We'll just be easy target practice for the Jerries!"

"Look, there aren't enough men from the forward company to do the job. I can give you one man who's been out there...he'll show you what he can. Your guys will have to do the rest."

I thought fast. "This is a goddam suicide mission. Listen, the part where I keep poking my way up front and getting shot...that part's getting a bit stale, you know? I've been trained for the mortar platoon. Hell, I was an instructor, back in England! If I take the guys out there and get the information you want, will you move me into the mortar platoon?" *I may live longer there,* I thought. *It's worth a try.*

"I'll look into it."

Yeah. Sure. I bet you'd say any bloody thing to get me out there. "Okay," I said. "I'll do my best."

"I know you will, Tommy."

Kiss my ass, I thought.

I went out with three of my guys and one from the forward company. The shelling was bad, and got worse. Then sniper fire took out one man. Naturally, it was the guide. He was dead. Bad for him, and also not so good for us. Now we didn't know where the *hell* we were going...and it was starting to get dark, as well. Before long, one of my men broke down. He started screaming—a drawn out wail like an English air raid siren. I couldn't blame him. He probably thought we were in danger.

"Mike," I snapped. "Take him back before he gets us all killed."

"You don't have to tell me twice," blurted Mike, and he started back at a cautious trot with his quivering comrade.

So then we were two.

"All right," I said (unenthusiastically, I admit), "I'm going forward. You coming with me?"

"Sure, I'll go with you, Smitty." It was Zeke. The Mohawk, remember? *Damn him to hell,* I thought. *Now I'll actually have to go! Shit!* I tried sneaking my leg out from behind the bit of cover we'd found, hoping to take a hit so the stupid Indian could carry me back to safety. *Better a bullet in the leg than dead,* I figured. No such luck. It just wasn't going to be that easy. We pushed forward.

But we couldn't go far. Before long, we were taking heavy fixed-line crossfire from three directions. The crack of sniper fire and the rip of machine guns competed with the thud of the shells that kept on falling all around us, and the acrid smell of cordite was so thick it clogged my throat. If we didn't get the hell out of there soon, we'd be catching it from all four directions and the game would be over. As soon as I was able to mark the positions of the main guns, we beat it back to our own front lines.

"It can't be done," I advised the adjutant. "Troops won't get through there without getting all shot to hell. A bloody *ferret* couldn't sneak through! Tanks could blast through, maybe..."

I could see he was disappointed. I wasn't too happy myself. It was hardly my finest hour. We'd accomplished approximately nothing, and lost the use of two men in the process—unless that noisy guy had stopped screaming and had a change of heart, but I wasn't counting on it.

And I think they sent the men in to attack through that death trap anyway.

All the same, a few days later I was switched to the mortar platoon. No more scouting patrols. The adjutant kept his word after all.

See...I saved the best news for last!

Finally (and it's about time),
Corporal Thomas Smith
Mortar Platoon

April 6, 1944

Kath,

Boy, what I wouldn't give for a field full of clean, white, Canadian snow!

Winter here has been one long, cold, filthy mud bath, hunkered down in waterlogged trenches under a mean grey sky. There are old guys who tell us that the hell of trench warfare in the First World War was a lot like this. Surely it was bad enough the first time. Who in hell decided we should do it again?

How do we keep clean? Well...we don't. Often the best you can do is to scrub your skin with your hands and hope to rub through the sweat, dirt and flaked skin to a relatively clean layer.

Socks are the worst. You can ignore a filthy uniform, but dirty, smelly, muddy socks can rot your feet. If we're sure to have the time to let them dry, any puddle will do to rinse them out a little. But wet socks are even worse for feet than dirty socks, and we can't afford to take the risk. So we stand them up by the fire. Yes, before you ask—it is not unheard of for socks to stand up entirely on their own! (Some of the guys are slobs...I have to admit it.) When they're quite dry, you crack them up well in your hands, pound out the dry mud, and then put them back on again. And some of the smell actually does disappear with the mud.

DODGING SHELLS

This technique probably won't catch on at home. I just thought you'd like to know. It's always good to have a backup option available.

Oh, it's not as if we never get to bathe. Hell no! Every once in a while the bath truck stops by...say, every couple of weeks or so (except when we're at the front—we could go a couple of months without a visit at the front.) When the truck arrives, they haul out rods and canvas and rig up a bath tent, with water piped in from tanks on the truck—hot water! Fifteen to twenty guys at a time strip down and stand in line for their turn to soap up, and they try to get rid of as much of the grime as they can scour off. It'd be a real treat, if the truck could set up anywhere close to us. But unless they want to give Jerry a free shot at our bare asses, the truck has to keep well behind the front lines and by the time we've marched all the way back there, enthusiasm for bath parade has petered out and we kind of wish they hadn't gone to the bother.

When we're not fighting, we practice, so that when we *are* fighting, we'll be really good at it. And we put in plenty of fun-filled hours keeping our equipment clean and in good operating condition...for the same reason. Guys who wouldn't pick a pair of dirty underwear up off the floor at home will polish their weapons until they shine. That gleam gives a comforting sense that the works won't fail us when our lives depend on it.

Scrounging for food falls somewhere between a duty and a hobby, and anything in a farmer's field that might add interest and substance to a stew pot is fair game. You'd be surprised at the feast some guys can cook up in a mortar ammunition box out of a bunch of vegetables, some bully beef and a can of steak and kidney pie. It might not pass muster in one of your better restaurants, but we're not too hard to please over here.

We're soldiers, and there's a war going on. So we take what we need. But we try to keep unnecessary pilfering to a minimum. The Italian peasants have a hard enough time already. We woke up to German gunfire one morning, after spending the night in a field near a ramshackle farmhouse. I saw the door swing open.

"Watch," I alerted the others. "Somebody's coming out."

"They'd better be bloody careful. The Jerries behind those guns might blink, and mistake them for one of us."

"I'll be damned! It's somebody's granny." An old woman in black tottered out. The whole country is littered with them. (There's always *somebody* to be mourning over.) Nothing threatening there, so we let her come.

"She's carrying a tray or something. What the hell is that?" When she got closer, we caught a whiff.

"By god...it's coffee!"

That old lady had risked her life to bring us what passed thereabouts as breakfast coffee! Nothing we could say would send her back till every man was served, and with a big toothless grin into the bargain.

She spoke a few words to one guy who knew a little Italian.

"She's grateful that we didn't steal what little she has left," he explained. "Apparently the Germans have been robbing the neighbourhood blind for weeks. She says she had to do what she could to thank us"

I never drank a better cup of coffee, and I doubt that I ever will.

Even water isn't always easy to find near at hand, and when shrapnel is flying, we aren't always eager to search very far. Not so long ago, we settled down near a small well, figuring that this time, at least, fresh water wouldn't be a problem. We had marched until we were exhausted, then we had marched some more. Sometimes the only way you can go on is to block out everything beyond the next footfall. You go into a kind of a trance, and concentrate all your will on putting one foot in front of the other, until somebody tells you to stop. You can't feel. You can barely see. I've seen whole companies of men trailing along in that state. Like zombies, in khaki.

It had been that kind of day. So each of us filled his canteen and flopped down to chug back a refreshing gulp. The guy next to me got a strange look on his face. Like he was trying to ignore something, and it wouldn't let him.

"Smitty...how's this water taste to you?"

"It's okay. Maybe a little...um..."

"Sweet?"

"Yeah...maybe a little."

"I wonder why?"

"Maybe there's something in the well."

"Like what?"

"How the hell should I know?"

"Maybe we should look."

"Why we? *You* look. I'm comfortable."

He hauled himself up and trudged over to the well. He peered down

"Shit!" he turned an interesting shade of green. "Shit! There's a dead guy down there!"

I spat, and coughed. "Well, *that's* not good. Hey, captain," I shouted. "There's a dead guy in the goddam well!"

"So get him out of there before anybody else drinks that stuff!" instructed the captain.

We hauled the body out—it was a German; we were glad about that—and cleaned out the debris as best we could. Then we dumped our canteens out and refilled them. The water still tasted kind of sweetish, and we wished it didn't...but we drank it anyway. We were thirsty.

I would never have believed that so much of my life could revolve around sleep. When we're fighting, or when we're marching, we often don't get any. We just have to go on and on, way past the point where we can't go on any longer. Maybe catch a few minutes, propped up in a trench or sprawled in a field...and back at it again. Then, between battles—when we've dug in somewhere for a while —there's nothing much to do *but* sleep. We have duties, but they can't fill the days and nights. So we try to catch up on the sleep we've lost, and hope to stockpile a mountain of it to draw on for the next battle...for the next march. This never works. Don't waste your time trying.

But sleep is our best weapon against boredom. And a soldier's life is boring. It's boring a *lot*. When we're not fighting or on duty, there's not a bloody thing to do. We only have what we can carry with us, and every damned inch has to be crammed with stuff that might save our lives. The odd worn out pack of cards...maybe a dog-eared book or two...we share those around. But mostly we slip our minds out of gear and just wait for time to pass. And when you come right down to it, every hour that passes is another hour we're alive. It could be worse.

Of course, we talk. We must talk...after all, these are my buddies—the guys who will try to save my life, if it needs saving! In some ways, we're closer than brothers. But it's an odd kind of relationship that requires no past, and can't count on a future. So we don't talk about the important stuff. Home, girlfriends, family—those are private things. We don't share those much. After all, why burden a pal with an extra load of memories that he may have to carry forward alone? So our conversations...well, they tend to be fairly uninspired.

"Did you see that girl in the last village we marched through?"

"What girl?"

"You know the one...the pretty one. She had a greenish skirt with flowers. She was standing by a cart."

"Nah. I don't remember any girl. What about her, anyway?"

"I think she was kind of, you know, looking around."

"Looking around?"

"Yeah, you know...*looking around*. I think she was available."

"Available for what? We weren't in that town for five minutes. We marched straight through, for Chrissake."

"Well, I bet if we coulda stayed longer..."

"You're an ass."

Sometimes, when we've been parked in some unremarkable mud hole for a while, we have even less to work with. So we have to fall back on old classics.

"Looks like rain."

"I doubt it."

"It could rain. The last time we thought it wouldn't rain, and it did."

"Oh...yeah. Well, I guess it *might* rain."

"Maybe not..."

We don't dare brood over our casualties too much; none of the Canadian platoons are anywhere near up to strength. It's safer to turn it into just another joke.

"They've sent up rations for a full platoon...are they kidding?"

"Shut up or somebody might notice. We'll each have double rations and a full belly for a change."

Reinforcements straggle in, but they're mostly raw recruits. They don't know enough about artillery yet and some of them have never even thrown a grenade. We veterans—the guys who've been fighting since Sicily—we try not to get too friendly with them. They rarely last long, and we have our own to mourn over. I guess we got old fast, because they seem so goddam *young*. We try to teach them, when we have a chance, so they'll stay on their feet a while, but some of the stuff you need to survive...well, it comes with experience, if you live long enough. They can't tell where shells are going to land from the sound, and they can't see where to take cover. Every field looks flat as a plate to them. Lob a shell at me, and I'll find a way to burrow into a *rabbit hole* if I have to! They're helpless under heavy attack, and then we have to risk our own lives trying to save them. It doesn't always work.

One thing is for sure...we can't trust them to cover our backs. They're simply not up to it. How could they be?

And they ask the most damn fool questions.

"What do you think will happen if we get captured?"

Easy. "I *don't* think about it." I suppose if I was wounded I'd be taken to a German hospital. If I was put in a prison camp, I'd escape. Who *thinks* about that stuff?

In case you don't know, a mortar is basically a big steel barrel propped up on a bipod, with the hind end stabilized in the socket of a heavy steel base plate on the ground. It will propel a 3" shell up to a mile and a half, and the shell is designed to explode on impact. It can do a lot of damage. The pounding as the shells leave the barrel slams against our eardrums—god help anybody who's prone to headaches—and the force of the shots can eventually pound that base plate into the ground deep enough that the trajectory has to be adjusted to compensate. I've seen guys stuff their ears with cotton to stop them from bleeding. The blasts can be that loud.

The mortars are transported in pieces on a Bren gun carrier.

You may as well know right now that Bren gun carriers are actually topless tanks that carry mortars, shells, and the mortar platoon. Or sometimes they pull anti-tank guns. They do *not* carry Bren guns; soldiers carry Bren guns. And there are no 'mortar carriers'. Don't ask why—it's the army!

The best thing about Bren gun carriers is…now that I'm not a Bren gunner, I get to ride on one.

Going into battle, each guy carries one piece of the mortar. The first guy dashes up and throws down the base plate (it has spikes on the bottom to bite into the ground). The next guy jams the ass end of the barrel into the socket and gives it a turn while the third guy fixes the barrel onto the bipod. The sight fits onto the whole thing…and we get it all done in a few seconds. We practice a lot.

A mortar, in the right hands, can be pretty damned accurate. Once it's assembled, we point it in the right direction, set the trajectory for distance, and fire a shell or two, correcting the aim till we get it right.

No one has to pull a trigger…the shells arm themselves when they hit a firing pin at the bottom of the barrel, and they're self-propelled…so if you're really fast (we're *really* fast) you can get over twenty shells in the air before the first one lands. That's over one shell a second…but you have to throw, not drop, those shells down that barrel…and you can't do it without skinning some knuckles.

DODGING SHELLS

Of course, you can only get that kind of speed in competition, not in battle. When the Jerries are shooting back at us, it puts us off our game a bit. I sometimes think they don't fully appreciate the beauty of the teamwork involved.

We were taking part in one of those speed competitions, throwing those babies down the barrel one by one, when something went wrong. One shell somehow must have gotten stuck on its way back up the barrel. It appeared at the mouth, and balanced on the rim like it was having second thoughts.

The bloody thing must be armed...and it's going to fall! If the nose of that shell hit the ground, there'd be nothing left of us but a crater in the dirt and a few spare parts. I watched that thing wobble there for...oh...it seemed like hours before I accepted the fact that I'd actually have to *do* something about it...or die trying. I was closest except for the loader, who still had the next shell in his hand, and nobody was pushing past me to save the day. We were set up on the brink of a steep incline, so as it fell, I grabbed the shell, shrewdly avoiding the nose, and heaved it over the edge. But carefully. Very carefully. It was as hot as hell from the charge, but believe me, there was no danger that I'd let it drop intentionally. Not if my hands were burnt off to the wrists! Over it went, and I didn't stay to watch it hit the bottom.

I'd like to be able to say that the shell exploded safely...that I saved the platoon that day. I'd like to say that, but in fact the damned shell *didn't* explode. Maybe, somehow, it hadn't gotten armed after all. Or maybe it rolled to the bottom of that hill without hitting anything at exactly the right deadly angle. We didn't follow it down to find out. We were just glad to be alive. And it was a generous five minutes before the other guys remembered the look on my face and started laughing about it.

The competitions keep us on our toes, and the infantrymen on the front lines count on us to mow down the Jerries who are firing at them, so it wouldn't do to slack off. On the theory that every detail counts, our weapons and even our transportation are inspected, and the sharper they look, the better the judges like it. As always, the Brits grab the best, the newest, the cleanest vehicles, and we're usually left to make do with whatever else is still mobile. But one time, we caught a break. Our carrier was in such miserable condition that it was being replaced, so we decided to pick the new one up in time to use it for an upcoming competition.

And let me tell you—it was a beauty!

I couldn't resist. "Hey, Mack," I said to the driver. (His name really is Mack.) "This is an easy road...let me drive for a bit. I could use the practice." He knew if anything happened to him, I might have to take over the driving. It's a war. You never know.

"Okay, Smitty," He climbed into the passenger seat. "But be careful. It's brand new...don't bend it."

We swung on down the road, and it felt good to be behind the wheel. *This is great,* I thought. *I must have a natural gift.*

"You're doing fine, Smitty. Turn left at the crossroad at the bottom of the hill. Look, when you're going downhill in this thing, you can brake, if it's easier...but it's better to gear down. Do you want to give that a try?"

Well, I had to learn, didn't I? It seemed like as good a time as any. As we started down the hill, I focused on coordinating my movements on gearshift and clutch. I started getting the feel of the thing ...gearing down smooth as silk. *Geez, I really look like I know what I'm doing.*

Whoa!

"Left! Turn left!"

The crossroad had snuck up on me while I was busy with the gears. I yanked the wheel left. Bren gun carriers are pretty manoeuvrable, so we turned the corner, all right, but the turn was too fast, and the weight of the vehicle swung it around wide and knocked the corner out of a stray house that was *much* too close to the road.

"Shit! Are you guys alright?"

"For Chrissake, Smitty! Yeah, we're alright ...but look what you did to the bloody carrier!"

The fender was all bent and scraped, and god knew what damage the foundation of that miserable shack had done underneath, where I couldn't see! I cursed all sneaky, devious Italian villages, and this vicious example in particular, and kept on going.

"Aren't you going to stop?"

"No goddam way! They're lucky I don't throw a grenade into that god-forsaken piece of rubble, just to clean up the neighbourhood," I sulked. I was feeling guilty for bending the carrier. And my driving skills were definitely going to be questioned. I could see it coming.

The competition was the next day, and I should have been resting up. But I spent most of the night doctoring up the wrecked carrier—pounding out the dent and slapping some paint on the fender. And for good measure, the guys helped me put on a new track, so the judges wouldn't see the scrapes. It wasn't exactly fresh out of the box any more, but it looked alright. Then I grabbed a couple of hours sleep.

The competition the next day tested our precision and speed in loading and firing. We should have won. We were an all-star group—we could set up, aim and fire a mortar in about 45 seconds. And we would have won, too...if I'd remembered to remove the damned barrel cap before ordering the loader to fire. The judges notice stuff like that.

I guess a couple of hours sleep wasn't enough.

Our captain, Big John, was a miner from Northern Ontario. He's a well-disciplined officer—a huge guy, with muscles in places where other people don't even have places. Big John demands performance...not protocol. He considers saluting a waste of time, and if we occasionally turn up with a choice piece of equipment that doesn't strictly belong to us...well, he doesn't ask for details. He's hard on the company—there's nobody harder. We train long hours beyond what's required for the battalion. That's what makes us so good. He doesn't care how we drink and carouse in our off hours—but god help us if we're not up at the crack of dawn, fit and ready to train.

DODGING SHELLS

Actually, most of our officers are fairly decent chaps. They dole out punishment when they have to, but I don't think they like it much. Most of the trouble I get into is just from raising hell or clowning around, and the officers understand that kind of stuff. They give me hell, then they give me something else to do—something that'll take my mind off my 'beef', or distract me from whatever mischief I've been brewing up. The crappiness of the chore depends on the gravity of the offence. Much like Grandma used to do when I was a kid, now that I think of it. I wonder if she's been giving them pointers.

Unfortunately, Big John has some unorthodox ideas. He's not content to stay behind the lines, where mortars are expected to be. No, that's way too passive for Big John. He sends us right up with the front line, so we can set up real close and give them immediate support as they go forward. Now, this doesn't fit in too well with my intention to stay back, out of Jerry's way. In fact, the noise and flash tends to draw the attention of the very Germans who would like us to stop, and have the fire power to make us do it. So we heap curses on Big John when we're in the line of fire, but we respect him all the same.

Of course, occasionally we do get away for a bit of rest and relaxation. During one of these interludes, I found myself (surprise!) in a bar, drinking with another corporal. I don't remember his name; I didn't know him very well. Gradually, a group of soldiers gathered—that tends to happen—and I listened while the guy told them how great he was.

He was the best...the fastest...the bravest...the smartest. Hearing him tell it, he was winning the war single-handedly. Anything they mentioned...he had done it, and better. After about half an hour of this, even the liquor couldn't keep them interested.

One of the group finally turned to me, to get a bit of a break.

"So, soldier...you've been quiet. Tell us about yourself."

"There's not much to tell," I said. "I'm the guy he just said *he* was."

Your modestly unassuming brother,

Tommy

June 3, 1944

Kath,

I finally got your last letter, and ours are starting to go out again as well. We've been incommunicado for a while. I guess you noticed.

Late in April, they began sneaking the whole damn Canadian army across Italy so we could throw a big surprise party for the Germans. No kidding. All Canadian radio operators gradually went off the air and, as far as the enemy knew, the Canadians seemed to have disappeared into thin air.

While we were on the move, radio traffic was being broadcast from various places where we *weren't*...in order to keep Jerry guessing. And any messages they did intercept wouldn't have been much help to them. It was way too tempting to aim them in all the wrong directions. I understand a few British soldiers here and there even sported the red patch, in order to throw them off the track.

I guess it worked. When we arrived in the Liri Valley, the Germans didn't so much as toot a horn to welcome us. We were dropping in, unexpected.

The Americans had been having some trouble taking Cassino. They'd bombed the town to rubble, but the Germans dug in and were using the remains of its medieval abbey to strengthen their line of defence—they call it the Gustav Line. From the valley, we caught glimpses of the shattered ruins on the top of the hill.

We laid low while thousands of barrels of burning oil sent clouds of stinking smoke rolling through the valley to cover our movements. We didn't want to give our position away before we were ready to pop out and yell, "Surprise!"

When we started firing on them, they knew the Red Patch Devils were back. And while the British and Polish troops chased them out of Cassino, we fought our way up the valley.

The Germans fell back behind the Hitler line, where they had put together a wide range of discouragements for us: mine fields and barbed wire, and an antitank ditch that they'd blasted across the entire valley. And artillery. A *whole lot* of artillery—craftily concealed so we wouldn't notice until it was too late. The guns they couldn't hide were protected by concrete and steel pillboxes, half buried in the ground, with slits so the bullets and shells could reach us conveniently. Those pillboxes might hold anything from machine guns to the turrets from disabled Panzer tanks, as well as the men who were firing them. And in case killing us in bunches this way didn't get us all, they perched snipers in the trees to pick off the survivors, one by one. The line was anchored on the west by the town of Pontecorvo, which gave the Jerries a nice, high, fortified spot to fire down from. They obviously hoped to stay, and we weren't invited in.

When they planned this death trap, they proudly named it for their Fuhrer. Then they started to worry that their impregnable line just might be breached after all. (Those pesky Canadians had a habit of raising hell every time they looked around!) So they, real quick, renamed it after one of their commanders.

No dice! We had planned to smash the shit out of the *Hitler* Line, and we weren't going to be cheated out of it that easily. We called it the Hitler Line...we *still* call it the Hitler Line...and I bet everybody at home does too.

In order to soften things up a bit, Allied planes and Canadian artillery bombed hell out of Pontecorvo. It went on for hours. We cheered them on.

"Will you look at that, Smitty?"

"There'll be nothing left of it but pebbles."

"Good. I don't like the damn' Jerries having a bird's eye view of us."

"I wonder if there are any civilians dumb enough to be still in there."

"I dunno. The smart ones are probably long gone ...but there are always a few stragglers left."

"Shit!"

"So, what then? You want to tell them to stop the bombing in case there are civilians in there?"

"Not a chance."

They sent the 48th Highlanders in alone to punch a hole in the Hitler Line, because they figured we could. We were short-handed—we're always short-handed—so the mortar platoon would be fighting right up front.

Of course.

I suppose the valley must have been beautiful before all this started. But I remember running crouched through a field of grain, hoping it would hide us from the Germans firing down from the ridge above the town. The oak trees and poplars that had been there were all splintered now by shell blasts and weren't much use as cover. It had been mined, of course, but we didn't slow down... there was no point. We had to get across fast, because if the mines didn't get us, the shells and bullets probably would.

The tanks had to cross the same ground, and they were a whole lot bigger. The mines we missed were there waiting for them, and they *couldn't* miss. I looked back and saw them scattered there, destroyed or disabled, many with treads blown right off. They'd tried, but they hadn't even reached the anti-tank ditch which had been cleverly fashioned from craters blown right across the entire valley to trip them up. We had to go on without tank support.

When we could get close enough to one of those pillboxes without being blown to smithereens, you can be sure we didn't charge in rashly. We preferred to throw in a phosphorous grenade, and stay the hell out of there for a while till the fire burned out. When we finally did go in to check, the Germans would still be there, all bloated and crispy and unlikely to be any further danger to us.

The shelling was brutal. When I struggled out of one slit trench where I'd hunkered down for a while, I found a solid circle of mortar craters within 20 feet around me. Jerry had obviously been using me for target practice. Lucky he didn't hit the bull's eye.

DODGING SHELLS

We *did* bust through the Hitler Line, and the Germans were definitely not pleased to see us. Nevertheless, when we saw that we were likely to be alone there with them for a while, we tried to make ourselves as comfortable as possible. We got all dug in on a ridge, kind of cozy-like, and we even had managed to get a supply truck and a Bren gun carrier through. Dan and I—I don't think I've mentioned Dan: a good guy, friendly enough—we were crouched in a dip in the ground about a dozen yards from the mortar pit, cleaning our guns, when the Germans decided that we'd been there long enough. We heard that horrible screeching sound again—I hate that sound!—and the seventy-five pound shells from their Moaning Minnies started slamming into the ground all around us. I knew we'd had it...they had our range, and the next one would land right on top of us. I threw myself to the left and tried to melt into the dirt. Dan threw himself to the right, flat on his belly. I was lucky. Dan wasn't. A shell hit the ground to the right of us, and a big hunk flew sideways, slicing right through him. The concussion from the explosion pounded me like a gigantic mallet.

I hadn't been wounded...but that concussion alone should have killed me. I must have grovelled just low enough for the main force of the blast to pass over me.

When I lifted my head and looked around, I understood exactly what had happened. I could see it all, quite clearly. A shell had hit near us. Very near. I could see the shell fragment lying there. Dan was dead...oh, definitely dead. I didn't really care much. I was alive. I didn't care much about that either.

And then...nothing. I have no damned idea what happened next.

I heard about it later.

"We were under terrific fire," one of the guys in my platoon told me. "We were all hugging the ground in the mortar pit, but I glanced up and saw you jogging over to us. You jumped in and sat there for a minute, like you were thinking about suggesting a game of cards.

" 'For Chrissake, keep your head down, Smitty!'

" 'Where's Joe Ward?'

" 'What?'

" 'Where's Joe Ward? Joe's out there...' You were looking out at the supply truck. It had taken a hit. Gasoline was leaking out of the tank and seeping into a nearby trench. I could see a guy lying in the trench, but he must have been dead.

"All of a sudden, you jumped out of the pit and ran over to that trench. You pulled the body out and stood there staring at it with a puzzled look on your face. We were all shouting at you to get the hell away from there! That gasoline was hot, and it was running all over the goddam place. It could have exploded any time! You paid no bloody attention...you just stood there, looking at the guy.

"There must have been a lull in the shelling, because we heard you say, 'Oh...this isn't Joe Ward! This is some other guy." You sounded kind of disappointed. "This guy doesn't have blue puttees...'

"Then you dropped the guy back down into that hot gasoline—and sauntered away, like you were shopping for socks, and you'd picked up the wrong size by mistake!

"It was the craziest fuckin' thing I ever saw."

I guess somebody finally pulled me back into the mortar pit, because I remember hearing:

"We have to get him to the hospital."

Who? I wondered, sluggishly. *Did somebody get hurt?* I sat where I'd been dumped, looking around quietly. I saw men running...shooting... *So this is war,* I thought. *I didn't know...*

When the medical jeep came around, somebody stood me on my feet, and told me to climb in. *A ride. That'd be good...*

"You can't sit there, pal." It was the driver. "You're sitting in my seat. Get in the back."

Oh. Okay.

As we drove away, I watched the shells exploding all around us, spraying dirt and shards of shrapnel against the sides of the jeep. The noise must have been deafening...but I don't remember any sound. Shell fragments were hitting flesh, and men were bleeding and falling all around us. Others threw themselves on the ground, scrabbling for cover. *Of course,* I thought...*because they might get hit.*

The driver looked scared. I wondered why.

I was fascinated. I seemed to be able to see every little detail, even through the smoke from the guns. It was like a really good war movie. *But it's so much more **real** up close like this.*

It must be terrible to be here, I thought. But it had nothing to do with me. I was only watching, that's all.

I wondered how I came to be on a bed in a tent, sweating and shaking. But I didn't care much. I tried to stop shivering, so the men around me wouldn't hear my teeth clacking together. The sheet over me felt clammy—with sweat, I guess—and was only pretending to keep me warm. I would have fought those men for another blanket.

They gave me something to eat and a cup of hot coffee. The part that I didn't spill warmed me up a bit, and I guess I must have slept because when I woke up, I wasn't shivering. No. But some jokester had slipped me the granddaddy of all headaches! Imagine a platoon of big, clumsy men in army boots bowling a game of ten-pins inside your head. It was a lot like that, but with nausea.

Padre East was there, sitting beside the bed and talking, talking...talking about...I don't know *what* he was talking about. I didn't want to hear it. I wished he would just go away. My mind wandered.

There's never bloody well enough to eat! Growing boys need to eat...how can we fight if we don't get enough to eat? Through Sicily, through Italy, I never have enough to eat.

"I've already had breakfast, Tommy." It was Padre East. "Have this." He handed me a plate of eggs.

"Thanks, Padre." I ate it. I knew it was his breakfast. I knew he hadn't eaten.

The Padre kept talking, yakking away, and eventually I started to listen.

DODGING SHELLS

"Tommy...I'm going back up to your company now. Would you like to come along?"

"I don't think so, Padre. No. I don't want to go."

"Well...I do have to get back there...could you just walk with me? I'd really appreciate it..."

I remembered those eggs...and I walked up with him. And I stayed. They told me if I hadn't gone back then, I would probably never have been able to go back. It was shell shock, and they say if you give in to it, you'll panic. I'd have been finished. I owe the padre a lot more than a breakfast.

I'm fine now. If the Germans thought they could finish me by rattling my brain, they didn't know their enemy. Now, if they'd aimed lower down, they might have been able to do some real damage.

Oh! Who was Joe Ward? You remember...I've mentioned Joe before. Joe was my buddy. But Joe was killed near Ortona...months ago. And the other guy? The guy I left in the pool of gasoline? Well, he was probably dead already.

By the time I got back, we weren't isolated any more. The rest of the Canadian army had fought through and the Hitler Line was finished. We'd done the job all right, but it hadn't been easy. It seems there'd been a few little flaws in the big plan. They said the British 78th Division would be protecting our right flank as we advanced. Where the hell were they? Apparently every artillery regiment in the entire Canadian Army had been over pounding hell out of a town called Aquino, to get the Germans out. We could hear the guns. We'd have been a lot happier if they'd been aimed in front of *our* platoon.

And the Yankees...weren't they supposed to be guarding our left? We'd seen no sign of them either. I guess they still hadn't managed to break out of Anzio. The only ones keeping Jerry out of our hair on the west had been the Moroccan Goums, fighting their way through the mountains. Those guys are good. They've kept up with us all the way.

As soon as we were on the move again, we saw plenty of evidence that the Germans weren't going to give up a damned thing easily. We had just passed a first aid post when we spotted a soldier trudging down the road towards us. He was a skinny, unimpressive guy, kind of slouchy, and he was dragging his feet a bit. He looked like he wasn't up to much. When we reached him, we stopped—it never hurts to find out what's going on up front.

"Hey, Mack...anything happening up there?"

"Yeah...you might say that. The Jerry bastards shot me. Then they held me prisoner...for about six hours, I guess. But they must have known you guys were coming, because they pulled out and left me there. There was no point lying there waiting for somebody to find me, so I started walking."

He straightened up a bit and we could see a line of five bullet holes right across his chest!

We had a clear view for almost half a mile up the road, and there had been no Germans there. So he must have been walking nearly a mile in that condition. Geez! The little runt was a lot tougher than he looked.

"So," he asked, "where's the first aid?"

"It's over there..." We pointed behind us.

"Good." And he walked on.

DODGING SHELLS

We were trudging through the ruins of a village, feeling pretty much as dusty and beat up as the buildings we passed, when I caught a movement out of the corner of my eye.

"Get a load of that!"

A young German soldier was stepping down out of the rubble into the road, with his hands in the air.

"It's a prisoner," muttered one of the older guys in the platoon. "So what? Somebody else is taking him in."

"Well, look at him! He must be about fifteen years old! What the hell's *he* doing here? He's just a kid!"

"Yeah…and you're nearly middle aged!"

"Shit! I bet he's never even shaved."

"Have you?" That hurt. I've been shaving for years. And it's a pain in the ass.

"Look at his uniform. He must have cleaned himself up for the occasion." He was spotless: tunic buttoned, cap jaunty—I guess he figured a helmet might indicate a certain lack of trust. I bet his boots had even been buffed up before he stepped out into that plaster dust.

He noticed us looking, and grinned, friendly-like. My hand automatically jerked up as if to wave. I turned it into a brow wipe.

"He doesn't seem very unhappy…"

"Hell…they're not stupid! They know they'll never win this thing. They just haven't found anybody with the guts to tell Adolph. Now junior will get to sit out the rest of the war somewhere comfortable. He's not smiling…he's bloody well laughing at us!"

Near dinnertime one day, we met up with a bunch of guys who had captured a small group of Germans that had been dug in on a rise overlooking the road. And they'd bagged a usable machine gun into the bargain. Their captain was inspecting the dugout, with his batman tagging along. We thought we'd mosey over and have a glance. The captain was checking out a dead Jerry officer sprawled out in there. He was gazing at the flashy big ring the guy wore…a heavy silver signet with a Nazi swastika.

I heard him say, "God…I'd love to have something like that!"

"So…" I suggested, "Why don't you take it? He doesn't need it."

"The hog's been scoffing too much wiener schnitzel—it's on too tight." He turned to his batman. "Look, bury this guy, will you? Then come down for your dinner."

We went back to the road, and settled down to eat. About fifteen minutes later, the batman appeared, with a big grin on his face. He handed the captain the ring…finger and all!

I hope the batman wasn't banking on making any points with that move. The captain turned greyish, threw the thing into the bushes and stumbled off to puke where it wouldn't disturb our meal.

It's a shame. That ring was a beauty.

DODGING SHELLS

The Italian summer sun is not friendly to dead bodies. We try to bury any corpses we pass—unless they're German and we're in a hurry—but there's no waiting list of guys who want the job. One poor bugger had died, slumped over the edge of a culvert. He must have been there a while, because the flies had found him and he didn't smell any too sweet.

"Alright...let's get him into the ground, guys," I suggested, cheerfully. We'd been drinking in the last town, and I was in a cheerful sort of mood. "You two dig a bit of a grave. And *you*...you get him out of the culvert and lay him out here."

Maybe the other guys hadn't drunk quite as much as I had. They were less cheerful.

"I'm not touching him! Look at those flies..."

"I'll dig, but he's too ripe...I won't touch him either. You do it."

"Kiss my ass! I'm not doing it. Do it yourself!"

Before a fight broke out, I decided to do the noble thing. "Oh, for Chrissake, I'll get him out of there!" I was really feeling no pain. I grabbed his arms and heaved.

That corpse made the most nauseating squoosh-ing sound I have *ever* heard. There isn't enough wine in Italy to drown out that sound. I dropped the body where it was.

"Cave the bank in on him." I said, and I walked away. It was a callous solution, maybe, but I can live with it.

So a word to the wise: if you're ever travelling through Italy, after this is all over, don't poke around too deep beneath the surface.

But if you do, and if you find that ring...I've got dibs!

Touring Italy the hard way,
Tommy

July 20, 1944

Kath,

We're on our way north, and the Germans have cleared out in front of us, so we're not meeting much resistance. We know they're up ahead, somewhere, but we're not chasing them right now, and I don't know why.

The soldiers on the line rarely understand why we don't go forward, if there's nobody with a gun or a tank in front to stop us. Oh, we enjoy the rest …but why not keep pressing forward until they're all gone? We just shrug our shoulders and pretend to believe that somebody up the chain of command knows what he's doing.

We still haven't seen any sign of the Americans. Weren't they supposed to hustle on over and cut off the German retreat from the Hitler Line? We thought so. But they say the Yanks beat it over to Rome instead, and let Jerry slip on past to where he can keep trying to trip us up. Seems like a bone-headed decision to us. I wonder how *their* troops feel about it. I mean…I guess they got to strut around in the city a bit, but it pretty well fell into their lap, so where's the glory in it?

I hear they posted signs saying "Rome Out of Bounds—Turn Back Now." I guess they meant us. Hah! Lucky we didn't go anywhere near there anyway, because there's bound to be lots of liquor in

Rome, and probably plenty of whores (sorry) so
some half-assed sign wouldn't have kept us away.

In case the folks back home are wondering, the
army does damn' little to encourage our drinking
habits (at least...the Canadian army. The others
are a lot more generous.) Maybe once a month or so,
when we come off a patrol or something, an officer
with a heart may issue a cup of rum and water. So
we're left to purchase or confiscate supplementary
liquid provisions for ourselves. This takes up a lot
of our free time.

We still don't talk about home much. In fact we
mostly steer clear of talking about the past at all. A
lot of us were so young when we joined the army
that we hadn't had time to have much of a life to
look back on. It gets harder and harder to remember what it was like before we were soldiers.

We don't talk about the future much, either.
What future? Most of us hadn't thought much about
it before we came over here—and we're not likely to
start now. Our life is all marching and waiting and
hiding and fighting. And for a break, we clown
around and do our best to get into whatever
mischief comes our way. What else is there?

The ones who've been fighting since Sicily
—we're professional soldiers now. When we're
fighting in the front lines we don't feel; we don't
even think, much. Our job is to survive and to kill,
and we're good at it. There's no morality to it; if we
don't destroy the enemy, they'll destroy us. We have
no mercy. We fight and kill to save ourselves—and
to get revenge for our fallen friends—and we keep

on killing until we're told to stop. In fact, when we're fighting, we become animals…and dangerous ones.

In case you were wondering, that's not nearly as much fun as it sounds.

The guys who've stayed alive here have learned to recognize the danger in the slightest sound, the smallest movement. We're suspicious of *everything*, and we know danger when it's anywhere nearby. But the truth is, all the skill in the world won't help you if you're in the wrong place at the wrong time. If we're still alive after a battle, we chalk it up to a lucky break—a thousand lucky breaks. Each one of us knows he could be next. You get used to that.

Of course, there are some guys who just can't take it. They quake and babble and weep, and they're hustled off behind the lines. We rarely see them again. I suppose they're shipped home, or they put them to work in the rear-area units where they're safe from everything more lethal than a hot coffee spill. The medics call it battle fatigue; the guys left fighting usually call it 'yellow'. I don't know…but I know I don't want them fighting beside *me*.

One day, the supply truck dropped off a bag of rice and a big sack of potatoes with our rations. Now, usually that kind of stuff stays with the field kitchen for the cooks to deal with, but we're always hungry and it's food and I got to it first, and I wasn't going to give it up!

"What do you want with that stuff, Smitty?" asked one of the guys.

"Are you kidding? Boiled potatoes...with rice pudding for dessert! What more could you want?" It may not sound like a balanced meal to you...but god dumped it into my lap and I was going to make the best of it.

"Who're you kidding? It's raw rice. In a bag. How's it going to turn into rice pudding? *You* gonna make it?" Was he mocking me? It sounded like he was mocking me. *I'll show him,* I thought.

"You're damn' right I am...I watched my grandmother make it all the time. I love rice pudding. How tough can it be? It'll need to cool before we eat it. I'll make it first. Then the potatoes."

"So, what do you need?"

"Well...I still have a can of condensed milk in my pack. That'll sweeten it up fine. And wasn't there a can of jam somewhere? Who's got the jam we didn't finish?"

Silence.

"C'mon! It's going to be a feast. Get the jam." I was beginning to make converts. The jam appeared. They were starting to hope maybe I could actually conjure up pudding.

"I'm going for some water. First guy to touch the rice or the potatoes gets a bullet in the head." They must have known I wasn't kidding, because when I got back with a helmet full of water, the sacks were still there.

Hardtack comes up to us in tins about 12 inches square, and we save them to boil up the water for our tea. I filled a tin over half full with rice, and poured in the water. Not right to the top—I left some room for the water to boil and the rice to fluff up a bit. The water boiled and I stirred and soon the tin was nearly full. The rice grains still looked raw. Bigger, maybe, but I could still hear them clicking around in there.

"I guess it needs more water," I admitted. "I'll go get some. Somebody stir the pot." Another helmet of water went into the tin, and some of the rice came out to make space. A bit of rice wasted, but we had plenty. No harm done.

I kept stirring...and the rice kept growing. It's like the damned stuff was alive! Soon the tin was full again, and it looked like cooked rice this time ...more or less. I checked a grain and frowned. Still not bloody well fluffy. More rice came out, and by this time there was a sizable pile of soggy, partially cooked grains mounding up beside the fire. The guys were starting to laugh. I dashed off for more water and when I got back this time, I noticed that nobody was tending the 'pot'.

When I started stirring, there were brown streaks in the rice...and a few black bits. Shit! It was burning on the bottom! I stirred more energetically (which didn't make the brown go away) and watched as the rice slowly crept up to the rim of the tin.

"It's done now," I announced sulkily. "Pass over the milk.

"Let me check," offered one of the braver guys. He tried a few grains. "Um...it's still kind of chewy."

"It's *not* fucking chewy," I said. "It's exactly right. Gimme the jam!"

"Not a chance!" It was a chorus: everybody at once...and still laughing. "The bloody rice is burnt

…and it's not even done yet. We're not wasting the jam on that slop!"

"Okay…so it's not pudding." I wasn't too eager to sacrifice my milk either, to tell the truth. "We'll eat it the way it is. Just take it off the top and you won't taste the burnt part."

"I'm not eating that," stated my brave comrade. "It's all burnt to hell! Dump it into the fire, Smitty."

"In a pig's ass! You're going to eat that damn' rice, and you're going to like it!" Their snickering was starting to get on my nerves.

"Or else what?"

"I've still got the potatoes! If that rice goes into the fire, the goddam potatoes go with it!" I was standing over the potatoes, and I guess I looked dangerous. They stopped laughing and ate the rice. Or at least, they made it *look* like they were eating the rice, which good enough for me. We're all pretty handy at helping a guy save face. When everybody is carrying a weapon, you learn to get along with others.

The potatoes? The potatoes were fine. Thanks for asking.

Our quartermaster is a grizzled guy with a hare lip and a short temper. We've all learned to avoid all comments about his…facial defect. At least, anywhere he might overhear us. It's a touchy subject, and he is the guy who distributes stuff. It's never smart to anger the guy who could give you the crappiest stuff.

Unfortunately, his job puts him on the phone a lot. And the phone connections are not great. It was bound to cause trouble sooner or later.

"Connect me to 455667," said the quarter-master. A reasonable request, but his hare lip made the numbers come out kind of nasal and blurry.

"I'm sorry," piped the operator. "Could you repeat that, sir?"

"I want 455667." It was just as muffled as the time before.

"I'm unable to understand your request," she said, in her most patient manner. "Would you please repeat that?"

"Four...five...five...six...six...seven!"
Frustration was mounting.

Bad line...speech impediment...she didn't stand a chance. "Sir, I'm afraid I couldn't understand your request." Ever so politely. "Could you repeat that, please?"

"Look," he sputtered, "Why don't you take that bloody phone and shove it up your ass!"

The story might have ended there, but she was British and she was insulted. (The British tend to be very sensitive to wounds in their dignity.) She lodged a complaint, and he was promptly ordered to apologize.

He placed the call. Orders are orders.

"Are you the operator I told to shove the phone up her ass?" Resentment coated the words like a prickly jacket.

"Yes," she replied, indignantly. "I am!" She'd been waiting for this call; the rude bastard was going to have to eat crow, and she wasn't going to make it easy on him.

There was a sulky pause.

"Well...you can take it down now."

W. L. BERTSCH

Always here for your reading pleasure,
Tommy

September 30, 1944

Kath,

We had a bit of a break as we moved north and west through the middle of Italy. There were no battles, but it wasn't exactly a vacation either, unless you get a kick out of sleeping out in the open. They say some guys do.

If you're picturing us lounging in camps with tents and other similar luxuries, you're picturing somebody else's army. We sleep on the ground and cook in the open and hope it doesn't rain any more than it takes to lay the dust. Who the hell would *choose* to do that?

By early August, we were outside Florence. The weather was beautiful—warm and dry—and we would have been happy to stay there a while longer. Eventually we expected to fight the Germans there, and it looked like easy going.

The Germans must have known we were there. They would have spotted our red patches—it seems like they were always watching for them. And just to make sure, I heard that some of the staff officers were pitching Canadian cigarette packages into the Arno where they could drift across and let Jerry know we were in the neighbourhood. Apparently we weren't counting on the element of surprise.

We took it in stride when the mortar platoon was ordered to prepare to fire on a German target across the Arno River. It seemed a bit rash to be digging firing pits in the middle of a field that would be in plain view of any German interested enough to stroll to the top of the intervening ridge, but we were accustomed to being put in difficult spots. The ground was hard as a rock, but what the hell...I didn't have to dig the pit. I had a crew to do that. I had something else in mind.

"Don't take any unnecessary risks," they told us. "It's risky enough already, digging out there in the open. And on no account wander over to that ridge." So I snuck over to check it out, of course. (Oh, relax. I wasn't the only one.) I wanted to know what we'd be dealing with.

"And if you do go up there, for god's sake, keep your head down. We don't want you to be seen, and you don't want to catch a bullet." I popped my head up to take a peek anyway. No point being there at all if you couldn't see anything, was there? I could see the city across a wide plain, with nothing much to worry about in between. So what was the big deal?

It took all night to dig the pits and stow the ammo. And at the crack of dawn, the order came:

"Break down the mortars. We're moving out!"

What the hell! It had all been part of an elaborately staged feint. We would have been seriously pissed off—we were ready to fight—but we *had* been pretty exposed there, and not getting shot at is always better than getting shot at. So we packed up and moved out...picking out the stitches of our red patches and insignia as we jounced along on the Bren gun carrier. The Canadians were disappearing again.

DODGING SHELLS

"Where the hell do you suppose we're headed now?" grumbled one of my guys. He was a bit grumpy—he'd been one of the ones digging pits.

"If they told us...it wouldn't be a surprise," I said.

"But Jerry's expecting us at Florence. And he always gives us such a warm welcome."

"So he'll be disappointed. We can drop in on him somewhere else. We'll give him a big, wet kiss, and all will be forgiven."

For the next week and a half, we joggled over the Apennines, crawling east-ish during the dark hours. By the end of the month, we were near the Adriatic coast again, ready to spearhead a jab at the Germans' Gothic Line over there. You can see the pattern, here. Every time we bash through a Line, they pull back and draw another Line. And we'd heard that Jerry had outdone himself in fortifying this one.

The little surprises they prepare for us are very orderly. For example, mines. They lay land mines —hundreds of mines—about five or six feet apart, and in a precise pattern. You'd think that would make them easy to avoid, wouldn't you? Like hop scotch, only deadly. And it would be...if you knew the pattern. We don't know the pattern. And they don't post a chart. I've looked.

Of course, I get to ride along the road with the mortars now, after the sappers have taped off a safe route. That's okay, I don't mind. Three wounds are more than enough, I figure. Risking more, when I can avoid it, would be foolhardy.

Oh…and we learned, from a captured prisoner, that the German paratroopers had rushed over to greet us again. We were touched.

There was plenty of lively action, even without skipping through minefields. Any building or haystack could be dangerous. As we approached one house, trading gunfire with German defenders inside, their shots sputtered to a stop.

"Look, Smitty," said one of my men. "I see them in the doorway."

Two German soldiers edged out. One waved something resembling a white flag.

"Don't shoot…they're surrendering!"

Something was wrong. I could see weapons.

"Hey!" I shouted. I'm just naturally suspicious —it's a character flaw. "Are you surrendering, or what? Put down your weapons!"

Their response was a burst of fire from two Schmeissers as they ducked back inside. The white flag lay in the dust outside the doorway.

"I guess not," I muttered. "Bastards."

You see? You can't trust anybody.

By now, the Canadians were spearheading the attack, and it's a fleeting honour we could have done without. We no sooner broke through the Gothic Line than the Germans retreated behind the Rimini Line. (I told you it was a habit with them.) More battles…more casualties…more prisoners. You get the picture.

Mortar shells are bloody destructive, and we often have to rely on phone instructions to make sure we're dropping them in the right places. Does it ever happen that we fire on our own side, by mistake? You're damned right it does. Mortar fire can be laid on to soften up objectives for the infantry, and the infantry is moving fast...as fast as possible. So we need that communication line open to make sure they're not moving right into the line of our fire. We don't want the wrong guys to die. It's bad business.

One time, we were shooting over a hill to protect fellows in a house on the other side. Of course, we had to be careful to shell the area around the house and miss the house itself. Hitting the house wouldn't have been helpful...I'm sure you can see that.

And how did we manage this little trick? Well, there was an observation post in a second house with a good view of the first, and the officers in that second house were directing our aim by telephone.

Since no shellfire was coming from the observation post, the men there were attracting little German attention. We, on the other hand, were loud and flashy and dangerous and very goddam noticeable. We continued to fire through the rain of shells from the German weapons, but pretty soon there were about thirty or forty craters a whole lot too close to us.

"Smitty, Jerry's got our range! We're in trouble here."

"Yeah, I know. We'll have to...*shit!*"

"What's wrong? Are you okay?"

"The bloody line's gone dead! They must have hit the wire."

We couldn't risk firing blind.

"Somebody has to follow this line up towards the observation post and fix it," I said. "Who's going?"

Every one of my crew appeared to be busy with something important that required them to keep their heads down.

"C'mon guys, somebody has to go. Maybe the wire's broken right around here somewhere." Even through the shellfire, I would have heard if anyone had whispered an offer. There were no volunteers.

I was right, though. Somebody had to go.

"Fine," I said. (It wasn't fine.) "I'll go." By now the shelling had almost stopped. The Germans must have figured we were all dead.

I started to run up the road toward the observation post, with the wire running through my fingers so I wouldn't miss the break. Once I found the damage, a quick strip and twist of the wire would repair it, and I could get the hell back where it was safer.

Wire's okay...wire's okay... The farther I ran the more dangerous it got, right out in the open like that. Finally I could see the house where the observation post was established. And I could see the break. A shell had hit the wire right outside the damn' door. Why the hell didn't they get out there and fix it themselves?

Probably because they didn't want the next shell to fall on one of *them.* There was a large yard around the house with no cover. And the shell that broke the wire proved that the Germans were at least aware of the location. Could I do what they wouldn't?

DODGING SHELLS

As I crouched there, by the low fence around the yard, I remembered a story I'd heard about a Russian soldier who'd been in a similar situation: broken communication wire...sent to repair it ...heavy shellfire. He repaired that line and the Russians won the battle. He was found (dead, of course...but I tried to ignore that bit) with the two ends of that broken wire clamped firmly together between his teeth! He was a hero. It was in the newspaper.

Well, I'd come this far...and I figured I was as brave as any Russian! And anyway, the shelling around the house seemed to have stopped for a bit. *I can do this,* I thought. I sprinted across the yard and grabbed the ends of the wire.

I heard yelling from inside the house. They must be cheering. I'd probably get a medal for this! *It's about time,* I thought. I gave the wire a twist.

"Shit!" I heard. "For Chrissake, get into the house, you bloody fool!" I stumbled through the door.

"You stupid bastard! You're giving away our position!"

I couldn't believe my ears. They were pissed off at me. Every last one of them.

"What kind of moron would pull a stunt like that? Unless Jerry's asleep at the switch, he's going to shell the shit out of us now!"

Well, fuck you! I thought, and I went to find a safe place to sulk. It was a farm house, of course, and a stone manger at the back exactly fit the bill...that was as safe as it was going to get. I crawled in and lay down with my helmet over my face, pretending to sleep.

That's it! I thought. *I'm done! Let 'em shell the hell out of this fucking house—I don't give a damn. You lot can fight the rest of this goddam war without me. A medal? Not bloody likely. The Russian guy...he gets in the papers...and I just get shit...*

By the time I woke up, most of the shelling had stopped, and the house was still standing. All the guys in it were still alive. As if I gave a crap.

I walked indignantly back down to my squad. They thought I was a fool for leaving in the first place. I could tell.

Of course, I got over it. It's hard not to get over that kind of thing when you see some of the stuff that happens to other guys.

We were passing by a guy sitting in a trench, in a lull after a heavy artillery barrage. The trench had been hit by a shell, and he looked a bit shaken.

"Hey, buddy," we asked. "Are you all right?"

"I need a cigarette," he said. He sounded pretty weak.

"Give him a cigarette, Smitty."

I lit a cigarette, and walked over to him.

"Here, pal."

"Thanks." He took a drag.

I knelt down and lit another for myself. I didn't know what else to do. I could see into the trench from there, and the shell had blown away all of him from the waist down.

There was no helping that guy. He wasn't even going to live long enough to want another cigarette. We do what we can. Under fire, if there's any hope of getting out alive, you'll often see a guy stumbling out of the thick of it with a wounded buddy draped over his shoulder like a sack of potatoes. If the shelling is too heavy, all you can do is pull the wounded into the nearest hollow in the ground and hope he'll be safer there till the firing is over and the stretcher-bearers can get to him. We'd do more if we could.

After every battle, we see the lines of German prisoners being brought away from the front. Some are young—really young—and a few of those are weeping like the children they were when they were dragged into this. They have no damned idea what's going to happen to them. But most look glad to be behind our lines, where it's safe.

We sat down for a smoke with the guys from another company who had captured a couple of prisoners.

"We were headed for our objective, and the gunfire from a bunker was holding us up," they told us. "We killed a couple of them and the others surrendered before we could pitch in a grenade. But we had to go forward. The rest of our guys were under heavy fire."

"So what did you do?"

"We told them to sit tight, and we went on up the hill. It was a bitch of a fight. After the position was secured, we stopped by the bunker for them on our way back down."

"You mean they were still there...waiting for you?"

"Goddam right they were! They wanted to get out of it as much as we did."

We're always surprised, after a major battle, to pass Italian peasants as we trudge along the roads. They're dressed in black, like scruffy crows, and are often trundling open cartloads of dead—adults and children—to the nearest cemetery. Those are the civilian casualties of artillery barrages.

We don't think about the civilians much. The smart ones leave before any big battle gets started. God knows why any of them stick around; I guess they have nowhere else to go. We can't help them. It's all we can do to help ourselves.

I doubt that they expect anything from us, anyway. We're ragged and filthy and bloody, and half dead with exhaustion. But we're still alive, and that's about all we care about for the moment.

We were fighting there for twenty-six days. We reached all our objectives. And the message has just been passed down to us from the commander of the British Eighth Army:

"Well done, Canada."

That's nice. I wonder if they'll stand us a drink. Probably not. Maybe there'll be something edible for dinner.

Still alive and still hungry,

Tommy

November 10, 1944

Kath,

You have to give the Germans a big gold star for stubbornness. We're still chasing them. They keep erecting one defence line after another, behind every ditch and stream. They don't even bother to name them anymore. They can't stop us; we keep moving forward...but at a crawl.

And we're crawling through mud! Rain has been falling in torrents. Bridges are being washed out (a serious inconvenience) and trenches and gun pits turn into swimming holes in no time. If it sounds like a bit of fun...it's not. One company was cut off by flooding for two days and reluctant soldiers had to swim a swollen river to get food to them.

It's rare that we can find a roof over our heads to keep the rain off. After a month of shelling, there aren't a whole lot of roofs left to be found.

So there's been no major breakthrough, but we're grinding them up, inch by inch. It's not easy. The bastards seem to be as strong as ever. We just have to be stronger.

And now...it's starting to snow! I don't mean a few catch-them-on-your-tongue isn't-this-fun fluffy flakes. It's *drifting*. I'm writing to keep my fingers from freezing. God help the next Italian who complains to me about Canadian weather. Sunny Italy be damned!

I suppose it could be worse. I heard that the German soldiers on the eastern front are being issued paper underwear this season. They say their long johns resemble leggings made of two thicknesses of crinkly paper. You know—the stuff bakeries tuck around iced cakes at Christmastime. Now, *that's* an idea that could never catch on in peacetime!

While I'm in a complaining mood...why the hell are we living on stuff the British army considers edible? Is there somebody in Canada who still doesn't know how bad British food is? And if we have to eat like the Brits, how come we only get a half a bottle of beer a month? The British troops get a bottle a day! How about copying *that*, eh?

I don't want you to think we have no entertainment at all, though. The Jerries do what they can to amuse us over the air waves. Their radio programming includes Lord Haw-Haw, who speaks English with a British accent and tries his best to keep our spirits up. Only yesterday, he announced:

"We know we have nothing whatever to fear from the Canadian troops. One third of you have been injured falling off motorcycles, one third are down with V.D. and all the rest are AWOL."

I wonder who he's relying on to do the research for those statistics...not the paratroopers, I hope.

I heard that the Russians have been running out of condoms. They sent a request to the British army for any that could be spared, specifying that they could only use the large size. Some comedian in Canadian stores got wind of it and did send them a carton of large condoms, but marked them 'small' and enclosed the following note:

DODGING SHELLS

"Here are all the condoms we can spare. Sorry, they are the small size. All the larger ones are in use by our own troops."

We've had more time to talk and to think lately. Is that supposed to be a good thing?

The married guys in our platoon (there are a couple) spend a lot of time talking about what things will be like when this is all over and we get home. The way they have it figured, they'll be lying in backyard garden chairs with cold beers in their mitts for the rest of their lives, with time out for a warm cuddle at night. But they know that those on-tap cuddles come with responsibilities. They worry about rounding up good, steady jobs when all the rest of us will be in the market too.

To tell the truth, we're not so sure we'll *ever* get home. The Germans are hanging on like grim death, and when we finally lick them, there'll be the Russians to deal with. (Seriously, who the hell trusts the Russians?) I figure if we can fight the Germans, we can fight anybody!

We've already managed to stay alive through a lot of really bad crap. We don't need to spend time guessing how long our luck will hold. So we mostly just talk about what might be coming up next…and hope it won't be too ugly. Ways to survive—that can always get a lively conversation going.

You've probably noticed that I haven't mentioned Alfie in a while. Well, Alf got shot in the chest while I was in the hospital in Africa, and he had to be sent home. He was gone when I got back. I miss the crazy bugger.

Most of the pals we started with in Sicily are gone—some dead, some wounded—but gone, anyway. We don't talk about that, much.

We heard there are about sixty thousand men in Canada who've been conscripted and trained, but can only be used for home defence. Somebody made them a promise, or something. Is there some secret threat looming over Toronto that you're not telling me about? Hell, the Jerries couldn't even cross the English Channel. How are they going to paddle all the way across the Atlantic, for god's sake?

They say the government is trying everything from bribery to blackmail to lure those fellows overseas so they can help us out here, but they're not buying it. Have they tried lollipops? How about trading cards?

Look, they really don't need to go to the bother. We call those guys Zombies and we don't want them here. We've got a job to do and it's tough enough already without having to babysit a bunch of shrinking violets. So let 'em sit at home and watch the scary skies for incoming sparrow hawks, or whatever it is they're worried about.

A little down, but nowhere near out,

Tommy

November 22, 1944

Kath,

I couldn't wait to tell you about my latest stunt.

Several weeks ago, word got around that married British soldiers who'd been away from home for three or more years were getting compassionate leave to go home and start a family. I guess they're afraid if this carries on much longer, there won't be enough Brits left to go home to.

"So they get to go home to shag their wives!" commented one of our wittier numbers. (No, it wasn't me.) "I'd be glad to do it for them. I could use a break. And I'd even give them a cut on the stud fee!"

"I hear they're favouring the ones with older wives…over thirty-five. Offer still open?"

"Sure, I'm not particular."

"Hell, we've been away from home longer than *any* of the Allied troops. When do *we* get a chance at that?"

And we didn't see why a married guy should get preference, either. A lot of those guys had gotten married right before they left England. What about the fellows who had left girlfriends behind? Why shouldn't they have a go as well?

After a few weeks, the rumours started to buzz again.

"You hear the news? They're going to start sending Canadian soldiers back home on leave—in time for Christmas!"

"Sure. Watch me holding my breath."

"No kidding! Thirty days at home…how about that!"

"Have they convinced Jerry to take a month off as well, then?"

"Not likely…so we can't *all* go. Only the first batch. The ones who've been here longest."

"Don't be a chump. It'll never happen. They're just stringing us along."

"Hell, we can dream, can't we?"

You've probably read about this stuff in the newspaper, but I guess you're not taking it any more seriously than we are. They'll never let us leave here as long as Jerry's alive.

Then, a couple of days later, I was out relaxing with a couple of the guys and a few bottles of wine. We were 'relaxing' rather heavily, I guess, and we cooked up a gag to perk up the day. When you're that 'relaxed', any little thing at all can seem hilarious.

"Hey, guys, Christmas is coming. Let's go home for Christmas!"

"Right. We'll hitch a ride with Santa Claus. Is his sleigh armoured? And if it is…how the hell do the reindeer pull the weight?"

"Nah…we don't have to do that. Remember …they're letting some guys go home…"

"Yeah, sure. Good luck."

"No, really. I heard how they're picking them. Anyone who's been overseas for five years could qualify. And they count double for time fighting in *this* hell-hole."

"Well, shit, we all qualify, then. We've been over here…since we were sober. That's *plenty* of years."

"And anybody who's been wounded three times qualifies. Hey, Smitty, you've been hit three times, haven't you?"

"Sure. So can I sell some of my years to some-body else, and still qualify?"

"What the hell…if I was making the rules you could!"

"You don't have to be married, do you? They won't make you get married…?"

"No, single guys can go too. You don't even have to *try* to start a family…"

"But you can if you want to?"

"Sure. If you want to."

"It'd be nice to be home for Christmas."

"Maybe we could get warm, at least. The weather back home can't be worse than this."

"I'm pretty warm right now."

"You're pretty *drunk* right now."

"Then they'll bring us right back here to our own company? I don't want to be stuck in with some other company…I *love* you guys."

"Yup. Right back here. Get off me, you drunken fool!"

"Well, I'm convinced," I said. "C'mon to head-quarters. Let's sign up."

"Don't you think we should wait till we're sober?"

"You likely to be sober before Christmas?"

"Not if I can help it!"

"All right then…let's go."

The rest is fuzzy, but I remember a young corporal trying to stop us at the door of the company HQ. I guess we looked a little under the weather.

"What's your business?"

"Stand aside, son," I snapped. (At least, I think it was snappy.) "We're six-year men, and we want to go home for Christmas! Where do we sign up?"

I think they let us all sign. I'm not sure...but it doesn't matter much. We know they'll never really let us go.

But it was a good prank.

Still a bit fuzzy around the edges,
Tommy

November 27, 1944

Kath,

You'll never believe this! I didn't.

A few days after my visit to HQ, one of the men stopped by as I was taking a smoke break. I figured he wanted to borrow a cigarette.

"Hey, Smitty," he said. "Big John wants to see you. Now."

I wondered which of my little larks he'd found out about this time. I guess it showed on my face.

"Relax," he said. "You're going home!"

"Yeah," I grinned. "Sure."

I jogged over to Big John's tent. *No point in aggravating him by dawdling,* I thought.

Big John looked up.

"You sure didn't waste any time, Smitty. Well, looks like you're going home for Christmas. Congratulations!"

I looked at him. "Right," I said. "What did you want me for?"

He laughed. "I'm not kidding. Your orders have been cut. You can leave right away. But there's something I wanted to talk to you about.

"You've been Acting Sergeant for a while now. But if you want to stay for a bit longer, I can get your rank confirmed as Sergeant. It should only take a couple of weeks. It'd mean more pay…"

It was almost as though he were serious. I grinned. "Piss off! I could be dead by then."

"Yeah," he said. "I see your point. Well, go sign the papers and get over to the motor pool to arrange for transportation to Naples. You can take the next ship out to England. They'll find another ship there to take you home. Merry Christmas...we'll see you next year."

Right, I thought. *I'll believe it when I see it.* I shook his hand and pretended it was on the level.

But I'm writing this on board a ship headed for England, so I guess...maybe they're letting me go after all.

December 8, 1944

When we got to England, we were sent to a holding unit near Guildford to wait until a ship was available—no one could say when. There were a few other guys from my unit, and we hung around waiting for a couple of days.

"It's driving me nuts, waiting around like this," I groused. "If I can get a pass, I'm going to visit a few of my friends."

"You have friends?"

"Very funny. I'll see you when I get back."

I had no trouble getting a twenty-four hour pass.

No ship was expected the next day, so I took an early train to Littlehampton and spent the day with some of my English friends there. I had to be back at camp that night. No problem. I'd checked the schedule. An hour before the train was to leave. I had a last brew, said my goodbyes and then sauntered to the train station.

"When does the train leave for Aldershot?" I could catch the last train to Guildford from there.

"Oh, that train's gone, sir."

"It can't be. Look at the time." There was a clock on the wall. I still had forty-five minutes.

"Yes...well, sir...the train left an hour early today."

The English!

"Oh, for Chrissake! So when does the next one leave?" This was going to leave me strapped for time.

"I'm sorry, sir. That was the last train to Aldershot today. There'll be another tomorrow at..."

I was starting to panic. "I can't *wait* till tomorrow. I have to get to Aldershot tonight! What's the next train that will take me in that direction?" By now I was shouting.

"Well, after midnight, there's a train to Basingstoke...it crosses the Portsmouth Road closer to Aldershot..." Now he really *looked* sorry. And a little scared.

"I'll take it!"

I slept in the station. I sure as hell wasn't going to miss *that* train. I only had a 24 hour pass, and I was already going to be late. I didn't need any more trouble than I was in now. I had to get back before dawn!

The train to Basingstoke was headed for the Canadian mental hospital there. I tried not to see that as an omen.

A sympathetic nurse on her way back to the hospital gave me some advice:

"This train crosses the Portsmouth Road much too far from Guildford. I'm afraid you have no hope of arriving before late morning. Perhaps you should come along to Basingstoke. I believe there's a mail van leaving for Aldershot sometime after three in the morning. They may be able to carry you along with them."

That seemed as good a plan as any. By then, I was getting really worried and having trouble thinking straight. There could be a ship waiting to leave for Canada already! Dawn. I had to get back by dawn!

When I left the train, I managed to bum a lift with the guys driving the British army mail truck.

"I'm going home for Christmas on the 'three wound scheme'." They were Brits. They didn't know anything about the 'scheme' but they understood three wounds...and they could see the five strips on the bottom of my sleeve that showed five years of service, so they agreed to take me along.

By the time we reached Aldershot it was after four a.m., and time was running out. I was still fifteen miles from camp.

"I have to get back by dawn."

"Sorry mate, you'll never make it."

"Even if I run?"

"Fifteen miles?"

"Sure."

"Can't be done. Not by dawn. Not if you was Jesse bloody Owens."

"Fellas, you have to take me to the camp..."

"Wish we could—really, we do—but this is as far as we go."

"But I'll miss my ship! We're leaving at dawn," I lied, "and I haven't seen my old mum in five years!

She's not been well..." (I would have said *anything* to get back before morning.)

That did it. They agreed to take me as far as Guildford, but that's the best they could do. And even that could bring them trouble. I ran the last four miles to the camp.

I pounded in just as trucks loaded with troops were pulling out...headed for the ship to take us home. But my kit! There was no time to get my kit!

"Hey, Smitty!" I heard a familiar voice from one of the trucks as it passed me on the road. "Over here!"

"My kit!" I gasped.

"We've got it here, buddy. Jump on."

I jumped. Good guys. They've always got your back.

While I'd been in Littlehampton, the other guys had gone into Aldershot to revisit a few of our favourite pubs, and they got a warm welcome.

You see, most of us had run tabs when we were stationed there, so thousands of pounds had been owed 'on tick' when we were transferred up to Scotland. The barkeeps were sure they'd seen the last of *that* money. They'd made a bundle of cash from us, so I guess they chalked it up to the cost of doing business with 'the colonies'.

But they had been surprised to find that, one way or another, all the debts had been paid off—all but twenty or thirty pounds—and they figured that was probably owed by guys who had died in action before they were able send the money back.

They liked the Canadians. We were a bit rowdy ...but they liked us just fine.

I was loafing around on the deck one day when a clean-cut lieutenant parked himself beside me and started to chat. He looked like he belonged on a billboard ad. He was a recruitment officer, on his way back from some kind of strategy get-together in England.

He didn't have a whole lot to say about himself, but he seemed really interested in my experiences. He did know all about the 'three wound scheme', and he didn't miss the five strips on my sleeve either...so I guess he knew I must have some stories to tell.

We had chatted for almost an hour when he dropped the bomb.

"Listen, you're a good soldier. When you go back, what do you think about transferring to the Pacific? It's looking like there'll be action there after the Germans are done. We need men like you over there. You could make a great career..." His voice trailed off. I guess he saw the look on my face.

"You must be bloody *kidding!*" I said. "What the hell's the matter with guys like *you* taking a few bullets for a change?"

I jumped up and strode away. We didn't speak again. I think he might have been offended.

You know, I'm beginning to think there may be an end to this thing after all. Once we clean up the rest of the mess, I'm thinking I may have to make plans for some kind of future. To tell the truth, I never thought I'd make it back, so it all looks like gravy to me.

I know I should have sent this letter from England, but I left it too late, then there was no time. But I don't know if it would have been allowed out anyway. The army is always worried that the Germans will intercept our mail. No sense handing them a free shot at blowing up a ship full of troops, I suppose. Hell, I guess I'll reach Canadian soil as soon as it would have, anyway.

I'll try to drop it in the mail as soon as we reach shore.

I can't wait to see you, Sis! And I'll be expecting to see a fatted calf on the table with the turkey this Christmas.

Hoping this isn't just a dream—or a *really* bad joke,

Tommy

Tommy arrived home in Toronto on December 15, 1944, in the aftermath of the worst snow storm Toronto had ever recorded. He still had that last letter in his jacket pocket.

The army had contacted his family, and his sister was at the train station to meet him.

Tommy never returned to Italy. After his leave was up, he was given a six-month tour of duty in Canada, and before that was over, the war in Europe ended...on May 8, 1945. Japan surrendered three months later.

He did not re-enlist.

In all, 93,000 Canadians served in the Italian Campaign. The elite German units who fought so hard against them developed a respect for these brave and determined foes. Over 25% of these Canadians became casualties and more than 5900 died.

But the campaign had succeeded in keeping 20 German divisions tied up and unavailable to oppose the Allies, as they launched the liberation of Western Europe and finally put a stop to World War II.

#

Other Books by This Author

Once More, From the Beginning
by Wendy Bertsch

The Bible is a delightfully preposterous book, with humour and outrages, like jewels, just waiting to be mined. Inspired by these nuggets, **Once More, From the Beginning** retells the Old Testament from a woman's point of view, exposing all the funny bits.

http://wendybertsch.com